HALE

a love story

K WEBSTER

"It was the eyes. The secret of love was in the eyes, the way one person looked at another, the way eyes communicated and spoke when the lips never moved."

—V.C. Andrews, *Flowers in the Attic*

DEDICATION

To my other half...I love you, heathen.

Warning
This book is an epic, emotional, raw love story…
between a brother and sister.
Many won't be able to handle that.
But if I don't tell their story, who else will?

He's my everything.
I would die without him.

Because he infects me.
My brother.
He's inside my mind.
My thoughts are black and bruised.
Twisted and wrong.
A secret that eats me alive, but one I'll take to my grave.

And then it happens.
He sees inside me.
Understands the darkness.
Loves what he finds.

I'm contagious.

It's true.
Now, he's sick too.

PROLOGUE

Hudson

Eighteen years old…

"**Y**ou're going," Mom snaps, her green eyes flaring with fury. "I won't hear another word about it."

I clench my jaw and glower back at her. "I'm a grown-ass man, Mom."

Her brown eyebrow arches in challenge. "And I'm still your mother. I will not have you throwing away your future for some girl."

Rylie is quiet from the living room as she texts someone and wisely doesn't join the debate. At fourteen, my sister likes to throw her opinion around like it matters. It doesn't fucking matter.

"But Amy and I are going to get married. I love her," I tell Mom, running my fingers through my hair in frustration.

Mom's gaze softens as she approaches. At thirty-eight, she's still young and pretty. Big green eyes that match mine exactly. Her lips painted a trendy matte red. "Your dad and I got married when I was just eighteen," she says, her lips quirking up on one side in a half smile as she thinks of my father.

"Exactly," I breathe out. "And you guys love each other. That could be me and Amy."

She lowers her voice. "I want more than that for you,

though. More than this." She waves around the aging kitchen of the house she and Dad rent out. "Three months and then you'll graduate high school. You have a full-ride athletic scholarship to the University of Arkansas. One of the best teams to play college baseball for, Huds. Don't throw all that away. Amy will still be here when you finish. Then, you can marry her and start your life once you have your college degree under your belt. Don't you want to have more than this?"

By more than this, she means always struggling to make ends meet. She works long hours at the hair salon and Dad kills his back working overtime each week at the machine shop. They're in debt up to their eyeballs and are trying to raise two kids. One who has psychological needs requiring therapists they can barely afford and the other one who plays high school baseball for the varsity team. We're expensive and yet they do what they can to provide for us.

Her jade-green eyes are teary and guilt tugs at my insides. All those practices she ran me to over the years. All the baseball equipment and uniforms and trips she and Dad didn't have the money for but somehow managed to fund. My entire baseball career wouldn't be possible without Mom and Dad.

"I just love her," I say, trying again, but my argument has weakened.

"But you may not in four years. I want you to experience life a little bit. Then, if Amy and you are still together, I wish you both the best."

Amy is going to be upset. Last night, I spent Valentine's Day with her and promised her I wouldn't leave once we graduated. She was so fucking sad. It broke my heart. Which is why I made the promise not to go to college when she begged me to stay.

No matter what I do, someone's feelings will get hurt.

But Mom is right. Without college, how will I be able to buy Amy a nice house and all the things she's used to? Unlike our family, Amy comes from wealth. Her dad is a family attorney and her mom owns a boutique in downtown Columbia, Missouri. Where I drive a beat-up pickup that Dad helped me fix up, Amy drives a brand-new Honda Accord. Our love won't buy us nice things. A college degree will.

"Okay," I concede, hating the word as it tumbles out of my mouth.

She walks over to me and hugs me tight. "Good boy. My good, good boy. You always make the right decision in the end. You have a good head on your shoulders like your father."

I pull away from her and give her a nod. "I need to break the news to Amy."

"Of course." She sends me an encouraging smile. "You're doing the right thing."

Then why does it feel so wrong?

ONE

Hudson

Three years later…

"**H**ale!" Coach Brass barks out. "My office. Now."

I groan and my buddy Nick laughs beside me as we dress. The locker rooms stink of a bunch of sweaty fucking guys who just killed it on the field. We're all a little rusty after a long winter break, but each of us is ready for spring training. This season we're going to smash Florida State.

"He's probably going to ride your ass for running like a girl," Nick says and nudges me with his elbow. I nearly drop my phone that has been buzzing nonstop.

"I still killed your time," I tell him with a smirk, pocketing my phone without checking it. Amy knows I have practice today. I don't get why she's been blowing up my phone.

"Whatever." He shakes his head. "We still going out tonight? Caitlin at Noggins will hook us up with free shit."

Because Caitlin wants his nut sack.

And her bartender friend, Jada, wants mine.

Last time we went, I got so wasted from the free shots the girls were getting us that I nearly fucked up everything with Amy. Jada had her shirt off, was in my lap, and her tongue down my throat before I finally snapped out of it and pushed her away.

1

Long-distance relationships are fucking hard.

I always see Amy when I make the almost five-hour trip north from Fayetteville to Columbia. We spend 90 percent of our time together fucking and making up for lost moments. But in between those times a few weekends a semester, I get lonely. Our Facetime chats usually end with her making me feel guilty in some way. Sometimes she can be such a nag.

"Hale!" Brass bellows. "I said now!"

His tone is sharp and not at all like the one he uses to razz on the baseball field. It unnerves me.

"Coming, Coach," I holler back and zip my bag closed. I shoulder it and amble through the locker room to his office where he paces. His back is to me and he runs both hands through his thinning hair.

Fuck.

Am I in trouble?

"Sit, son," he says, his voice cracking slightly.

Son?

Something tells me this isn't about baseball. My job then? I've been working at Mrs. Brass's accounting firm on the days I don't train. Since I'm getting my degree in Finance, I get to mentor under her while making a little bit of money in the process. I'm saving up to get Amy an engagement ring.

"I was sick last Friday," I lie. "If I messed up on someone's return, it's because I was sick." Really, I was nursing that hangover and the mountain of regret I had from making out with a girl who wasn't my girlfriend.

He turns and regards me with sadness gleaming in his eyes. I slump into the chair, hating his expression.

"Coach…"

"Have you talked to your sister, Hudson?"

Hudson?

Coach always calls me Hale.

Fuck, this isn't good.

I furl my brows in confusion. "Rylie? No. Why?"

"Son…" He pauses and pain flashes in his eyes. Pity even. "She's been trying to get ahold of you. Then she called me."

What did she say to him?

Irritation bubbles up inside of me. My sister sometimes is every bit as bad as Amy. Always wanting to know when I'm coming back home. Griping about Mom and school and whatever else seventeen-year-olds bitch about. She's an attention seeker and when my parents aren't showering her with it, she demands it from me. It's times like these, I'm glad I left Missouri. "No, what does she want?" I groan in frustration.

He sits on the edge of his desk and his Adam's apple bobs as he swallows. "It's your parents."

"What about them?" Bile rises in my throat, but I swallow it down.

He pinches the bridge of his nose and shakes his head. His nose turns slightly red and his nostrils flare. "They were…" Tears form in his eyes as he swallows down his emotion. "I'm sorry, son, but there's no easy way to tell you this. They were killed in a head-on collision this afternoon."

I blink at him in confusion. "What?"

"I'm sorry, Hudson."

"Rylie is just making up bullshit again," I snap as I rise from the chair.

He shakes his head as he rises and walks over to me. His palm clasps over my shoulder and he squeezes it. "You need…you need to call your sister." Then, he grimaces, blinking away tears. "Go home. Take as long as you need. The team and myself are here for you."

This isn't real.

This isn't fucking real.

I yank my phone from my pocket, jerk out of his hold, and ignore all the missing calls and texts from every god-damned person I know. Instead, I call Mom.

"Hey, I'm not available to take your call at the moment. If you're booking for February's Valentine's cut and color special, please leave a message and I'll get back to you."

It beeps and I growl, "Tell Rylie to fucking stop. Call me back."

"Hudson—" Coach starts, but I wave him off as I call Dad.

His deep voice that sounds much like mine rumbles through the line. "Leave a message."

"Dad, Rylie is pulling some shit. Call me."

I hang up and my phone rings in my grip.

Rylie.

Infuriated, I swipe it to answer. "Whatever bullshit you're—"

A loud, ugly sob rings in my ear. Heartbroken. Terrified. Soul-shattering. Tears instantly burn at my eyes as I shake my head.

"N-No," I choke out.

"D-Dad is…" Rylie trails off as she gags through her tears. My heart races as my own tears slide down my cheeks. "He and M-Mom…t-they're g-gone."

"No, Rylie," I whisper. "No."

She just cries. "I d-don't know w-what to do."

I swipe my cheeks with the back of my hand. "Call Aunt

Becky and Uncle Randy. I'm on my way."

"Okay," she croaks out.

I hang up and stare numbly at my coach. "They're dead."

He pulls me to him for a hug. I've never embraced this man in my life, but I cling to him as my world crumbles beneath my feet. As though he has the power to fix it.

Truth is, nobody can fix it.

When the pained sobs stop rattling from me, I find the strength to pull away and stare at my coach. His face is bright red and his cheeks are stained with tears. I imagine heartache is written just as plainly on my face as well.

"I need to go," I rasp out, swiping at my tears with the heel of my palm.

His lips press into a firm line. "Take as long as you need, son."

They're dead.

They're fucking dead.

I pull into the driveway at nearly one in the morning. Dad's truck is in the driveway, but Mom's is missing. Aunt Becky's Lexus is parked behind Dad. I climb out on shaky legs and start toward the house.

I'm numb.

I don't even really believe it.

A part of me hopes it's one of Rylie's stupid games. That I'll walk inside and Dad will be asleep on the couch, snoring loudly. But when I walk through the front door into the house that smells like Mom's snickerdoodle scented wax warmer, I don't see Dad. I find Rylie's head on Aunt Becky's lap. Aunt Becky's face is bright red from crying and her hair is disheveled.

It's real.

Rylie's eyes open and when she sees me, she bursts from the couch. I'm nearly knocked over by my little sister as she hugs me fiercely. I squeeze her tight against me, the emotion locked in my chest escaping with a ragged sob of my own. Together we cry at the loss of our parents.

Since Rylie was a toddler, she's always been my annoying little sister. As she got older and started having issues, we drifted further apart. It seemed as though she was always trying to make life hard for Mom and Dad. While I was working my ass off to make things easier for them, she was upsetting them at every turn.

But none of that matters at the moment.

Right now, all we have left is each other.

Aunt Becky rises from the sofa and walks over to us. She hugs us, whispering assurances like, "Everything's going to be okay, kids."

Will it?

My heart sure doesn't fucking feel like it.

"Is this a bad dream?" Rylie asks, tilting her head up. Her pale brown eyes are the exact replica of Dad's. It makes my heart hurt to see them.

"No, Ry. I'm sorry."

More tears roll down her cheeks and she buries her face against my chest. All I can do is hold my sister and hope Aunt Becky is right.

TWO

Rylie

Four days later…

I stare at their bodies. First Mom and then Dad. They look like wax people. Not real. Dad has rosy cheeks, for crying out loud. If he knew the funeral home put make-up on him, he'd lose his damn mind. The thought of him sitting up and swiping the blush off his cheeks has me giggling.

Inappropriately so.

"Rylie," Hudson warns, irritation in his tone.

He stands near Mom's casket and adjusts her hair so her bangs aren't hanging over her closed eyes. She doesn't look like herself either. The way they styled her hair is reminiscent of some bad eighties music video. If she wasn't dead already, she'd die of a coronary.

I giggle again.

"Rylie," my brother hisses, shooting me a sharp glare.

I swallow down the laughter because people are arriving to view the bodies. What kind of sick society do we live in where this is a thing? Mom and Dad don't even look like the people we knew and loved. And yet here we are staring at their unmoving corpses and whispering things they cannot hear.

It's stupid.

Where are you, Daddy? Where did you go when you left this body?

My questions go unanswered. They always do.

"How you holding up?" a sweet voice asks.

Without looking up, I know the voice belongs to Amy Kent. My brother's longtime girlfriend. Her perfume fills my nostrils and I try not to shudder.

"Fine," I answer and finally glance at her.

Her shimmering blond hair has been twisted into a modest bun. The simple black dress she wears is demure but can't hide the fact Amy is curvy. Blatantly, I stare at her breasts, no doubt double Ds, and wish I were blessed in that department. Mom used to say the Hale women didn't need big boobs. We had big smiles instead.

I'm not smiling now.

I'm wishing for bigger boobs.

At my parents' funeral.

Amy hugs me from the side, squishing me with her big boobs. I wonder if Hudson is obsessed with them. She's somehow kept my brother on a leash this entire time and it's not because of her winning personality.

A grin tugs at my lips.

"There's my girl," she coos. "Your parents would be happy to see you smiling."

I look past her and meet my brother's annoyed green-eyed stare. My smile falls. The disapproval in his eyes is overwhelming sometimes. I get it. He's the golden boy and I'm the fuck-up. The end. Hudson is the Hale kid who'll go off and do great things while I'm left here pondering the meaning of life. Sometimes I think God made a mistake. Accidentally stuck me on this earth when I was better suited for some dark hole of existence.

Amy beams up at me.

It's too damn bright here.

Turning away from her supportive smile and my brother's bothered glare, I reach forward with my thumb and attempt to wipe away the blush on Dad's cheek. His skin is cold and gross feeling. As soon as I touch him, I kind of wish I didn't. But now that I realize the red is coming off, I'm invested in seeing it through to the end.

"Cheer up, Ry-Bear."

Those were the last words Dad spoke to me. I didn't understand why they had to have an anniversary dinner without me. I was their kid. If they had just taken me with them, I'd be lying in a third casket finally knowing the meaning of life. I'd be dancing somewhere in the dark. Alone. Happy. At peace. Hudson would have to fret over the fact they'd want to pluck my thick, dark eyebrows because I've told him before bushy brows are the style now and he'd want to honor that. He'd tell them to take me out of the boring dress they'd no doubt put me in and let me wear my favorite red flannel shirt I stole from him before he went off to college.

Someone sobs loudly and I laugh at them.

I laugh until I realize it's me sobbing.

I'm a mess.

"Cheer up, Ry-Bear."

Amy tries to hug me, but I push her away from me. Dad looks like a girl right now and I need to fix it. His lips are tugged into a permanent frown.

"Cheer up, Daddy," I whisper, my tears splashing on his face as I see to it he doesn't get buried looking more like a woman than Mom.

"Rylie," Hudson warns, his body heat behind me, letting me know he's close. "Stop it."

Ignoring him, I rub and rub and rub, the tears blurring Dad before me, until I'm being pulled away by strong arms.

I kick and flail and scream, but my captor is too powerful. I'm dragged into a private, side room and the door closes behind us.

No longer able to fight, I collapse in Hudson's grip. Thankfully, he's strong enough for both of us. I'm unable to carry on with a brave face like he does. Aside from that first night, I barely see any emotion from him. He's able to compartmentalize his feelings. It's unfair.

I clutch onto his suit, no doubt smearing Dad's makeup all over it, as I cry against him. My brother and I have always fought, but right now he's the strength I need. He hugs me fiercely. His mouth whispers promises that he'll always take care of me. That together, we won't be alone.

God, how I want to believe him.

But as soon as this funeral is over, he'll pack up and leave us. He'll leave his dead-inside sister and his big-boobed girlfriend. I'll be left to pick up all the pieces while he throws the ball around and makes America proud.

My heart that aches so badly starts to go numb. The numbness trickles through my veins and bleeds through each nerve ending. I'm as good as alone.

"Everything will be okay," Hudson vows, mimicking Aunt Becky's annoying mantra. His words send a flare of anger surging through me.

"No, Huds," I bite out. "It won't be okay. Our parents are fucking dead."

He winces and looks over his shoulder as if he's embarrassed by my words. The same reaction as always. Any time one of his friends or coaches or another parent might see his obnoxious little sister act out, he'd look over his shoulder. With a furious growl, I shove him away from me.

Despite being much taller than me and carrying at

least a hundred pounds more than my small frame, he gets caught off guard. He stumbles and nearly falls on his ass. Anger blazes in his green eyes as he storms over to me. His fingers bite into my biceps as he clutches me.

"Calm the hell down, Rylie," he snaps.

I try to wriggle from his hold and shove him again, but he yanks me to him. His strong arms lock me in a hug I can't get out of. My big, mean brother holds me and continues to whisper assurances to me.

For a moment, I believe them.

Together, we believe his lies.

But nothing will ever be fucking okay again.

Ever.

THREE

Hudson

Three weeks later…

"Y ou should let me rub the tension from your shoulders," Jada says, her smile bright and flirtatious.

Nick nudges me with his elbow. "Yeah, Hale. Let Jada rub one out for you."

"I'm fine," I tell her, forcing a smile.

She waltzes off and I do allow myself to check out her ass. God, I'm a fucking prick. My phone buzzes and it's like Amy has a sixth sense of anytime I even think about another girl.

Amy: Can you talk?

I type out my response with one hand and knock back a shot with the other.

Me: Studying. I'll call you tomorrow.

Amy: I miss you.

My eyes lift to meet Jada's blue ones as she leans forward to pour more tequila into my shot glass. Her big tits are all but spilling out of her shirt. Maybe I find myself attracted to Jada because she reminds me of a naughtier version of Amy. Blond hair. Big blue eyes. Tits that would make most men achingly hard over.

That's it.

I just miss Amy.

"Thanks," I grind out as I reply back to my girlfriend.

Me: I miss you too.

Emboldened by the liquor, I press her.

Me: Show me your tits, baby. I miss them too.

She sends me a bunch of wow-face emojis.

Amy: Don't be a perv.

No pictures of her tits.

Me: Come see me.

Amy: I wish, but you know how my mom gets. I have to open the boutique tomorrow. When can you come back home?

"After my shift, a bunch of us are heading to the lake. Want to come with me?" Jada asks, her full lips turning up on one side.

My dick sure as hell wants to.

"He does," Nick answers for me. "Just don't tell his girlfriend."

Jada smirks. "Your secret is safe with me."

Amy: ??

Me: Spring Break in a couple of weeks. Headed to bed now.

I pocket my phone. "I guess I'll go."

This was a bad idea, but as we all sit around the bonfire laughing and cutting up, I can't help but relax. Since Mom and Dad died so suddenly almost a month ago, I haven't found many moments to enjoy. Baseball feels forced. School is a drag. My job with Mrs. Brass no longer keeps my interest. Even Amy gets on my nerves. So having a chick flirt with me and hold her own on baseball stats is kind of fun.

"We could get out of here," Jada says, a playful smile tilting her lips.

"Last time we left the herd, I made out with you. I have a girlfriend." The frustrated way I say those words is pathetic. It's almost as though I wish I didn't have a girlfriend, which is nonsense. I love Amy. I'm going to marry her one day.

Right?

My mom's words echo in my head. It was almost as if she knew I'd reach this point. I wish she were here so I could talk to her about it.

"I heard about your parents," Jada says. "I'm sorry."

I jerk my head up to find her staring softly at me. "It's fine."

"It's not, though. You have to be hurting." She grabs my hand and squeezes it. "I like you and would love nothing more than to help you not hurt."

My cock aches at her insinuation.

But then my phone buzzes in my pocket, reminding me once again I have someone back home.

Rylie: I can't take this anymore.

Frowning, I tug my hand from Jada's and reply to my sister.

Me: Take what?

Rylie: Aunt Becky! She's a Nazi! I hate her.

God, she's so fucking dramatic.

Me: You'll live.

Ignoring my sister, I pocket my phone and rise from the log I was sitting on. Jada stands too. I can't say the words, but it's like she knows anyway. With my head down, staring at the leaves covering the earth, I walk to my truck. When I reach the door, I don't get to open it before two slender arms wrap around my middle from behind. Jada's fat tits press into my back and I close my eyes. Then, her palms roam south. She cups my erection through my jeans and I let her.

I fucking let her.

"Jada," I growl. "I can't do this."

"You don't have to do anything," Jada purrs as she turns my body.

I lean against my truck door as she pulls at my belt. My dick has thickened and throbs for attention. Amy and I had sex last time—once—when I was down for my parents' funeral. It had been rushed and borderline angry on my part. And quite frankly, it was the best sex we've had in a long time. Even if I did make her cry.

"It was like you were mad at me."

Guilt is rattling through me, knocking at every bone in my body. I should push Jada away and call Amy. That's what girlfriends are for. You lean on them when shit in your life is overwhelming.

"It's not about you. I'm just upset."

A groan hisses from me when Jada releases my cock from my boxers. Fuck. I need to stop this. What about Amy?

"I know you're hurting, Hudson, but you don't have to be hateful."

Amy's selfish words are forefront in my mind as I search for a justifiable reason for what I'm doing. Warm lips wrap around my cock and my eyes close. I try to imagine it's Amy so I won't feel so fucking horrible, but all it does is remind me Amy doesn't give head anymore.

"The taste makes me gag."

Jada bobs on my dick and I'm dizzied from the pleasure of it. I feel like I don't know what the fuck is going to happen anymore with my life. One moment my life was all planned out for me. The next moment, it all feels so uncertain.

"When you do it from behind, it makes me feel like I'm a whore."

Images of the last time I fucked Amy spring back into my mind. After the funeral, I'd taken her to my old bedroom, bent her over the bed, shoved her dress up, and fucked her fast.

Jada runs her tongue along the tip of my cock and I groan, "I'm going to come."

She opens her mouth and closes her eyes as she strokes my cock faster and more furiously. For a moment, she could pass for a sluttier version of Amy. I grunt as I climax, my semen splashing all over Jada's pretty face.

I'm relaxed and happy for all of three seconds.

Then reality slaps me in the face.

I just cheated on Amy. I let a bartender with a nice rack suck my dick.

Fuck.

I wake up with my back stiff and my chest hollow. Last night was a mistake. A lapse in judgment. It shouldn't have fucking happened.

The morning air is cold and Jada shivers beside me. She wasn't offended when I cursed and then bitched about what a mistake I made. Simply told me to get in the truck and let it out. With virtually a stranger, I let out every damn thing that was bothering me.

My parents' death.

My nagging girlfriend.

My bratty sister.

I felt like such a spoiled little shit as I griped about people I'm supposed to love and care about. But, fuck, if it didn't feel good to get it all off my chest. Jada, being the good bartender she is, talked a little and listened a lot.

Thankfully, we didn't do much more than that.

I can only take so much guilt for one day.

"Want to go for breakfast?" Jada asks as she sits up and rubs at her neck. In the broad daylight, I can see she's not as pretty as Amy. Not that I ever thought she was.

God, I'm so stupid.

"Nah, I have a class in an hour," I say as I turn the engine over. "I'll run you home, though."

She buckles her seatbelt and regards me with kind eyes. "Last night was just a stress reliever, Hudson. Don't ruin your life over it. You should probably try to unpack some of that stress more often. I'm always here if you need help." She winks at me, insinuating she's always down for a blow job.

"Thanks," I grit out as I drive away from the lake.

The entire ride to her apartment, she tells me of her family and other things I don't actually hear. I nod politely and answer when asked questions. And when I finally drop her off, all I do is wave. When she's long gone, I pull my phone out and plug it into the charger. As soon as it comes to life, I see I have missed texts and calls from everyone.

My heart sinks.

Last time that happened, I learned my parents fucking died.

Amy: We can Facetime. I'll show you my boobs.
Amy: You really did go to bed.
Amy: I love you.

I scrub at my face and growl. I'm such a fucking idiot. All the texts on my phone are from last night. While I was getting my dick sucked by some random girl.

Rylie: You don't understand. They hate me.

Rylie: Did you listen to that song I sent you? Reminds me of Dad.

Rylie: Mom and Dad used to take us to Lake of the Ozarks each summer. Will we still go or did all our traditions die with them?

Rylie: I was looking through some boxes in Aunt Becky's basement. I found the one with Mom and Dad's wedding pictures. You look just like her.

Rylie: It hurts, Hudson. It fucking hurts.

Rylie: I miss you.

Rylie: Fuck you too.

Not only did I cheat on my girlfriend, but I let my sister down too when she needed someone to talk to.

Aunt Becky: Can you call me when you get a chance?

Aunt Becky: I caught your sister smoking pot in the basement.

Aunt Becky: She is out of control. Call me.

I'm overwhelmed this morning, but I dial my aunt anyway. She answers on the first ring.

"Hudson," she greets, her voice icy.

"Hey, Aunt Becky."

"Will you please talk some sense into her? Randy and I can't get through to her. She threw her phone at the living room mirror. I'll be vacuuming glass out of the couch for weeks now. Weeks, Hudson. And if she thinks I'm buying her another phone, she has another thing coming."

My phone buzzes and I grit my teeth. "What do you want me to do, Aunt Becky?"

"Here," she blurts out. "Talk to her."

"Hello?"

"What?" Rylie snaps. Her tone is angry, but I hear the underlying sadness in her word.

"What the fuck is going on, Rylie?"

"Aunt Becky is crazy," she hisses. "She thinks just because she's rich and I have to live with her she can control me. I don't want her money!" She screams the last sentence.

Aunt Becky screams something back.

"Calm the fuck down," I bite out. "She's doing her best."

"Whatever, Hudson. Go do your thing. Bye."

She hangs up on me and I pinch the bridge of my nose. Class time comes and goes as I sit in the parking lot of Jada's apartments. I pull up the song Rylie sent. "Stuck in the Middle with You" by Stealers Wheel. As soon as I hear the folksy tune, it does remind me of Dad.

Amy: I missed my period.

Goddammit.

Leaning forward, I rest my head on the steering wheel. I can't deal with this shit right now. I can't fucking deal. Ignoring my girlfriend and everything that text implies, I turn up the music and think back to days when Dad would pluck away on his acoustic guitar and try to sing songs he had no business singing.

I miss him.

I miss them both.

Fuck.

FOUR

Rylie

"Come on," Aunt Becky snaps as she parks in front of the drugstore. "I'm not leaving you out here alone."

She probably thinks I'll steal her precious Lexus. Rolling my eyes, I climb out of the car and follow her into the building. We're going to be late for school this morning, but when are we ever on time? The school must be tired of me too because they keep writing off my tardies and absences as "still coping with parents' death."

There is no coping.

Just the death.

It's a constant thought in my mind. Each morning when I open my eyes, every night when I fall asleep, and every moment in between. They're gone.

Aunt Becky leaves me to go to the pharmacy. I browse up and down the aisles. Maybe I'll steal something just to piss her off. I'm smirking when I run into another girl. She drops a pregnancy test at my feet.

I bend down to pick it up, but before I can look at her, she speaks.

"Hi, Rylie," she clips out.

Snapping my head up, I stare at Amy's red-rimmed eyes. "What's this?" I demand as I wave the box in front of her.

She plucks it from my grip and nervously looks over her

20

shoulder. "None of your business."

"Are you pregnant?" I demand, my voice shrill.

"I missed my period," she snaps. "I don't know."

All I can think about is Hudson. Mom's wish for him to finish college and worry about Amy later. She's sure on the fast track of reeling him back home. And as much as I'd love to have my brother closer, especially now, it pisses me off.

"You can't do this to him," I blurt out.

Her eyes widen in shock. "Do what?"

"Trap him," I hiss. "Have you ever heard of birth control?"

She gapes at me, tears welling in her blue eyes. "What's wrong with you?"

That's the million-dollar question.

Everything.

Everything is wrong with me.

It's why we're in this stupid pharmacy in the first place. Aunt Becky thinks she can fix me with meds.

"Don't do this to him," I plead, my voice choking up.

Amy scowls. "I can't exactly help that now, can I?"

"You could end—"

"Rylie!" Aunt Becky hollers from the end of the aisle. "Let's go. You're already late."

"I would never do that," Amy tells me, her bottom lip wobbling. "Never."

"No," I spit out. "Because all you think about is yourself."

Storming away from her, I push past Aunt Becky and run out the door.

Away. Away from everyone. Away from it all.

∽

I stare at the bottle of pills on my dresser. Same old dresser, new room. When my parents died, I was uprooted from my home and moved into my aunt and uncle's place. Aunt Becky was horrified when I chose to bring my own furniture into my room rather than use her fancy stuff. Mom and I spent last summer sanding down all of my old furniture I had since I was a kid and repainting it. It's kind of shitty because we both sucked at restoration, but it's one of the few things we did together and had fun.

If Mom knew Aunt Becky was trying to shove all these pills down my throat, she'd freak. Mom was always so into holistic healing. Even when the doctor diagnosed me as bipolar, she assured him that through therapy and family support, I'd manage just fine.

I was managing just fine until they died.

Now, I'm spinning and spinning.

I hate my school. I hate this house. I hate everyone.

I especially hate Hudson.

He's off living the perfect life with a probably pregnant girlfriend waiting on him. In another year, he'll finish college and come back home to marry Amy. They'll probably have ten kids and live in a fancy house next door to Aunt Becky and Uncle Randy. Meanwhile, I'll still be Rylie, the one who can't get a fucking grip on life.

Unscrewing the lid to the bottle, I inspect the pink and white pills. Lithium. I'm supposed to take this magical pill and I'll become normal. So Dr. Livingston and Aunt Becky say. It's going to take a lot more than one pill to make me normal.

I don't need these damn things.

I told my aunt that.

I just need my mom and dad.

With a grumble of frustration, I storm into the bathroom, ready to flush them all down the toilet. That'll piss Aunt Becky off. I'm just about to do it when I catch a glimpse of my reflection.

Daddy.

Same soulful light brown eyes. Same dark brown hair. Same smattering of freckles on my nose and cheeks.

Tears. Tears. More tears.

That's all I do these days.

Rage and cry. Rage and cry.

Nobody fucking cares either. Not like Mom did. I was frustrating to her, but she tried. Researched new things all the time in an effort to help me. I loved her for wanting to help me in a way that didn't feel like she was taking over my life. But the one who helped the most was Dad. He was funny and seemed to always be relaxed. It relaxed me too. I know his job was hard and it hurt his back, but he'd come home and give me all of his smiles.

The girl in the mirror, who looks like her daddy, cries.

Some days, I wonder if I even know her anymore. Some days, I don't know this person who fills her body. Some days, I feel so lost.

No one will ever find me.

Maybe I do need fixing.

But it will take more than one pink and white pill.

The girl in the mirror must know the secret to happiness because she swallows them. Gags and gags and has to use water from the sink. But she swallows them. All of them. She wants to be fixed.

And me?

I clutch the side of the sink, nausea crashing into me like a giant wave. I'm going to throw up. I splash cold water on my face, but it doesn't help. I'm sweating and dizzy.

I wonder if I asked Hudson his secrets to happiness, would he tell me?

Would he say, "Rylie, you just have to not be a fuck-up. Easy."

And would I say, "Ahhh, now I understand."

I'd be normal just like my brother.

I could be an aunt, a much better aunt than Aunt Becky, to the little baby in Amy's belly. I would spoil it and whisper secrets to it. Tell it exactly how not to be a fuck-up.

"Easy," I would say. And the baby would understand.

Unlike me.

The baby wouldn't have to crawl behind in his brother's shadows his entire life, trying to be good enough. The baby would start life with the upper hand.

I would help the baby.

The baby would thank me.

The room spins and bile comes up my throat. I barely manage to reach the toilet before I'm retching. All the normal pills splash into the toilet, splattering my face with gross water. I'm reminded that my happiness can't be fixed with a pill or thirty. My happiness is something that sits in the bottom of the commode, just waiting for someone to come flush it all away.

Blackness crawls around me, threatening to swallow me under.

To flush me down along with those happy pills.

If I could talk to the blackness, I'd say, "Take me."

And it would.

But unfortunately, I can't talk to blackness. My happy pills don't get to make me happy. Brothers don't tell their sisters the secret of life.

In my world, I exist alone, surrounded by people.

A nightmare. A paradox. A harsh sentencing for a crime I didn't commit.

Blackness swarms around me like a cloud of angry bees. It stings inside and out. All over.

Blackness doesn't drown me, it poisons me.

⁓

Machines beep and I try to open my eyes.

So dark.

So warm.

Not alone.

A strong, warm hand grips mine tightly, pulling me from my dreams of bees and unhappy pills. I blink my eyes open.

Sharp green ones bore into me.

Accusing.

Angry.

Achingly beautiful.

The sickness I always keep drowned below the surface thrashes to the top. It always grabs onto me at the worst possible moments and threatens to drag me under. For one moment, I let it take me. I admire his handsome face that resembles mine. Let my eyes linger on his thick lashes. Let them slide down to his strong nose. Let them fall to his full lips.

His lips move as he hisses out furious words, but I don't listen to them. The bees buzzing in my head are still too loud. All I can do is focus on the beauty in front of me. A beauty I've secretly adored since I was a child.

Sick. Sick. Sick.

No matter how many sessions with Dr. Livingston I've had, I never tell him what infects my innermost desires. Even I know some things are better left unsaid. It doesn't stop him from prying and snooping, picking apart my brain as though it's a bowl of candy and he's searching for the only green M&M in the bowl.

Sick, Rylie. You're sick.

My eyes droop but not before I push away thoughts of green M&Ms and green eyes and carefully guarded secrets.

"Rylie."

His voice, though, speaks a language only my sickness understands. It reaches out to him. Begs to be held. Spreads and spreads and spreads.

"You stupid, stupid kid."

The sickness retreats as fire chases it away. I pop my eyes open and glare at him. My brother. My nemesis. The one I'll never be like. I try to move my lips, but nothing comes out.

"Get some rest and when you're better, we're going to talk." He rises from the chair beside the bed in the sterile room. My eyes track him as he walks over to Amy. They hug. I wonder how he feels knowing he's going to be a dad.

Tears leak from my face, but nobody sees.

Nobody ever sees the pain that bleeds from my body day by day.

They go about their lives thinking only about themselves.

Closing my eyes, I seek out the darkness. The bees. The pain. I just want to think about something else.

When a warm thumb rakes across my cheek, I snap my eyes open. Hudson stares down at me. Pain, much like the pain I feel a slave to inside, flickers in his eyes. My big, strong older brother is suffering.

"We're going to talk about this. We're going to talk about a lot of things," he murmurs.

I watch him leave with his perfect pregnant girlfriend latched onto his arm. More tears leak out long after they're gone.

What will we talk about, Huds?

Will you tell me the secret cure for the sickness in my heart and the blackness in my head?

Of course not.

Hudson doesn't share his secrets.

And neither do I.

FIVE

Hudson

"**W**e could always try, though," Amy says, a sweet smile on her face. "For a moment there, as I peed on the stick, I was hoping I was pregnant. Can you imagine how cute our babies will be?"

I stare at her, numb. "Yeah."

"Only one more year. Maybe after the summer, we could try. Then, by the time you graduate from college, we'd have a little baby. I wouldn't need a big wedding, Hudson. We could get one of Dad's friends at the courthouse to marry us." She beams at me from across the table.

"I need to go," I mutter as I stand and toss some money beside our empty plates. "Rylie gets out today."

Her features crumple and her bottom lip wobbles, but she simply nods. Sometimes I wish she wasn't so fucking compliant.

"Okay," she says with false cheer as she slides out of the booth. "Let's go get our girl."

I stop her with a hand to her shoulder. "I think I need to spend some time with her." Alone. I don't say that word, but I imply it with the look I'm giving her. I don't like upsetting Amy, but she's so clingy at the worst times. Rylie almost fucking died the other day and Amy's planning babies and shit. My sister tried to commit suicide. I've lost half my family already. I can't lose the only person I have left.

"I see," she replies, tears shining in her eyes. "I'll just walk back down to Mom's shop. Go on and get your sister. Maybe I can stop by later tonight and see you guys. How are Becky and Randy anyway?"

"Fine. Yes, that sounds good. Thanks, babe." I pull her to me and kiss the top of her head. Remorse for what I did to her hits me hard in the gut. I need to tell her about Jada. That I let some girl suck my dick because I missed her.

This could all end.

But would it?

Amy is too forgiving. The moment I tell her, she'll cry and cry, but then she'll try to fix us. That makes me feel even worse.

"Talk to you later," she says as she pulls away and exits the restaurant.

Relief floods through me in her wake. I'd freaked the fuck out when she told me she might be pregnant. The test proved she wasn't and then the next day she started her period. At least I dodged one bullet in my life.

My mind is a mess. Right now, I should be in class. I should be getting ready for this week's ball game. I should be worrying about my future with Amy.

Instead, I'm driving to a hospital.

To pick up my sister.

I get distracted on the way by thoughts from the past.

"I'll call you after rehearsal is over," Amy says, standing on her toes and brushing a kiss over my lips.

I flash her a smile and then leave her near the choir room door to seek out Rylie in the freshman hall. I'd rather hang out and watch Amy sing with her choir buddies, but Mom insists I get my sister home from school each day when I don't have practice.

The freshman hall has long emptied out and I don't see Rylie sitting in front of her locker waiting like usual. Unease flitters through me. She's always waiting. If she's off making out with some boy when she's supposed to be getting ready to go, I'll be pissed. I want to go home and change clothes before I take Amy out to dinner tonight. I don't have time for this shit.

I'm passing Mr. Wright's room when I hear him bitching someone out. I shake my head because that guy was such a dick when I had him in the ninth grade. I'm glad I don't have to deal with his pompous ass anymore.

"Your attitude stinks," he snaps. "What do you have to say for yourself, young lady?"

I stiffen because I don't like the way he's talking to a girl. Everything in me calls to keep hunting down Rylie, but I take pause to eavesdrop.

"It's not attitude," she says softly. "I've just been having a hard time lately. I'm sorry."

My hackles rise.

Rylie.

Not just any girl, but my damn sister.

I turn on my heel and storm into the classroom, fury bubbling up inside me. Mr. Wright stands in front of her desk, towering over her. I used to fucking hate how he'd exert his height and power over people.

"Is there a problem here?" I demand, gesturing at where my sister sits with her head bowed.

She jerks her head my way and relief flashes in her eyes. It's enough to have me wanting to yank Mr. Wright away from her. Instead, I fist my hands.

He tilts his head to the side and pierces me with one of his stern glares, not moving from where he stands too close to my sister. "None of your business, Hale. Go on and wait in the hallway."

"Absolutely not," I say lowly and take a step toward them. "I want to know what's going on here and why she's in trouble."

He clenches his jaw and glowers at me. Several of Amy's friends think he's hot because he's not even thirty yet and fit. But he's a massive asshole. I don't like the way he talks to Rylie.

"Rylie here," he states as he points his finger in her face, "was sleeping in class and when I confronted her, asking her why, she shrugged at me. She's disrespectful and rude, a trait that is clearly common in the Hale family."

I stalk the rest of the way over to him, loving the fact I'm taller and bigger than this prick. He glares up at me, clearly furious that I'm in his space. I could kick his ass if it ever came to it and he knows it. Using my intimidating stature, I back him away from my sister several steps.

"If you have a problem with my sister, call my parents. I won't have you bullying her."

His eye widen and his mouth parts. "I wasn't—"

"So she's free to go?" I interrupt, the challenge hard in my stare.

"I'll be calling your parents," he growls. "Get her out of here."

Rylie is already standing by the time I turn and regard her. She rushes over to me and clutches onto my arm, much like she does when something scares her. That fucker scared my sister. I want to turn around and deck him, but I know my mom would shit bricks if I screwed up my scholarship. Instead, I guide her out of the building and into the warm spring afternoon outside. We're silent as we make it out to my truck. When we reach the vehicle, she stops. I turn my body to face her.

"Thank you," she utters, her cheeks turning pink. "You didn't *have to do that."*

"Nobody fucks with the Hales," I tell her with a lopsided grin. "Especially pervy assholes like Mr. Wright."

"He's probably just mad because I don't flirt and tell him how amazing he is," she mutters and rolls her eyes. "I swear, he gets off on having a bunch of teenage girls giggling over how hot he is. For the record, I don't think he's hot." Her lips tug on one side. A rare Rylie smile.

She wraps her arms around my middle and hugs me. My sister may get on my nerves sometimes, but I still have the overwhelming urge to protect her from idiots like Mr. Wright.

"Why were you sleeping in his class anyway?" I ask, my chin resting on the top of her head. "I overheard you talking. You're depressed right now? Why?" I don't understand her illness, but I want to.

Her body tenses. "My mind is just a mess lately."

"Care to share?"

"Not this. Not ever. Not to anyone."

The memory fades but the guilt remains. She's always been suffering and I've never been man enough to put the time in to help her. Always someone else's problem. Certainly not mine. Looking back, I wish I had listened to her and tried to help more. God, I feel so fucking terrible.

I'm pulling into the hospital parking lot.

To pick up my sister.

Because she was so sad and upset and lonely, she tried to overdose.

All I had to do was talk to her. Instead, I blew her off to get my dick sucked. When I park and head toward to the hospital, Aunt Becky and Uncle Randy are walking out. Rylie walks between them. Pale and broken. So fucking broken.

"Want to ride with me?" I ask her as I approach.

Her eyes lift to mine. Light brown like the coffee I had at the diner. But coffee never looked so fucking hopeless. "I guess."

I motion with my head and Aunt Becky flashes me a grateful look. Walking over to my beat-up truck, I open the door for my sister. She's slow in her movements but manages to sit inside. Her fingers shake as she reaches for the seatbelt.

"I've got it," I assure her, my voice gruff with emotion.

I tug the belt and stretch it across her tiny frame. So many times I buckled her in for Mom. This time feels different. I'm not helping my parent with my little sister. I'm having to *be* the parent for my little sister. The thought hits me hard and I shake it away.

My world is shifting on its axis.

Responsibilities are moving this way and that.

A deep sense of protectiveness over my sister settles over me. She's always been a nuisance. A bother. Someone whom I resented because she didn't try. Now, I see it's more than an attitude. Her brain is wired differently. The pain I've seen lately in her eyes is real. So real. A living, breathing organism inside her. Something that if I knew how to lure it out of her, I would. I'd take it and kill it. I'd free my sad sister of the way it suffocates her from the inside out.

The truck starts and R.E.M. starts playing, "Everybody Hurts." She sniffles from the passenger side as we drive. When I reach for her hand, she doesn't pull away. With strength that surprises me, she squeezes my hand. As though I've thrown a raft into the choppy waters she's been drowning in. The way she clings to me has me vowing nonverbally to the both of us that I'll be a better brother to her. I won't let her suffer alone. Not anymore.

Our fingers link and I don't let her go.

The Hales are strong because we have to be.

When we arrive at Aunt Becky's big house, I let out a sigh as I shut off the truck. Rylie stares out the side window. The pain we both feel over the loss of our parents is a never-ending punch to the gut.

"We should get inside," I utter.

"Don't go." She turns her teary gaze my way. "Please."

"I'll stay for a while," I promise. Coach will be upset I miss the game against Oklahoma State, but this is more important.

She smiles at me. Brilliant and happy. A smile I don't fucking deserve.

"Thank you."

I'm gutted at how one simple statement made my unhappy sister smile again. The depression eats at her day by day. Yes, I accuse her of being dramatic. No, I don't believe that's the truth. I've lived with her depression our entire lives. It's something I can't manage or control, so I choose to hate it instead. I treat it like it's something she can just get over, knowing full well she can't.

My expectations are unfair.

I'm an asshole.

She's quiet as I help her out of the truck and into the house. I guide her to the refinished basement where Aunt Becky said I'm free to stay anytime I'm in town. I've unpacked some of my things from the old house but mostly, it's filled with boxes of our memories. Rylie doesn't ask to go to her room. She clutches onto me in such a desperate way, I realize just how much I'm needed.

Completely.

We sit down on the sofa and Rylie curls into me, seeking my comfort. I hug her to me. I inhale the familiar scent of her hair and try to whisper to her soft assurances. Promises that I hope fill her heart up.

"I'll be more present."

"You can talk to me whenever and I'll answer."

"You're the most important thing to me."

"I'm so fucking sorry."

"I love you, Rylie."

With each word that tumbles from my lips, she relaxes. I don't relax until her soft breathing fills my ears. She sleeps, clutching onto my shirt like I might run away in her slumber. I cover her hand with mine and kiss the top of her head.

"I'm not going anywhere," I murmur.

Not yet.

Not for a few more days.

Hang in there, Rylie.

I wake up in the pitch-black darkness soaked in sweat. I'm covered by a slight body and a heavy blanket. I manage to grab hold of the blanket and pull it away from us. Aunt Becky must have tried to help. Suffocating us is not helping.

I'm on my back, sprawled out on the couch with my shoes still on, and Rylie sleeps glued to my front. When I run my fingers through her hair by accident, I notice she's sweaty too. But when I try to push her away, she whimpers.

Such a sad fucking sound. Like kicking a kitten. Despite sweating my balls off, I hug her to me. We're a mess of hot, sticky limbs, but at least she's safe. This time, I run my fingers through her hair on purpose. I mimic the way Mom used to do. It always soothed my sister, who suffered mentally all the time. And now, just like always, she relaxes.

I'm awake now and my mind races to find solutions to problems. A mental search for cures and answers. But all that running and running in my head turns up nothing.

Twisting, I shift our bodies so she's between me and the back of my couch. I stifle a chuckle when she grips my shirt tight. It's a little cooler this way and I find myself drifting back to sleep. I don't stop stroking her hair. I want her to feel safe and loved. Without Mom and Dad, it's up to me. I realize that now.

I won't let you down, Rylie.

—❧—

"Go away," I groan and toss my pillow at my sister, who stands in the doorway to my bedroom.

She huffs as she dodges it. "But the weatherman said—"

"We never get tornadoes, Rylie. Do you even hear any sirens?"

Bad storms are common for Missouri, as are tornadoes, and it's just something you learn to live with. Rylie has never been a fan, though, and always tends to stress out over them.

"No, but…" Her bottom lip wobbles.

"But nothing. We're safe. Besides, Mom will be home in another hour. You'll be fine."

Her shoulders hunch and she exits my bedroom. A twinge of guilt niggles at me, but I push it away. She's nearly fourteen and overreacts to everything.

Still, I can't quite get over the fact I was being a dick to her when she was scared. Technically, I'm in charge until Mom or Dad gets home. I should be doing what I can to calm her fears. Just as I decide I'll go make some frozen pizzas to distract her, I hear them.

Softly at first.

Then, the wails grow louder and persistent.

Tornado sirens.

I jolt off the bed and run down the hallway, calling out to my sister, "Rylie!"

She rounds the corner and launches herself into my arms, sobbing. "I told you! I told you!"

Panic seizes me and my heart beats nearly out of my chest. I pat her back as if that has the power to soothe me as well.

"Shhh," I murmur. "We'll sit in the bathtub and it will blow over. We'll be fine."

"I wish we had a basement like Aunt Becky."

"I know," I tell her. "Me too."

She clings to me, her tears soaking my neck, as I rush into the bathroom. With my little sister holding on to me like she's a koala hugging a tree, I climb into the small tub and sit down. Her body is tense and she trembles.

I stroke my fingers through her soft hair and listen for sounds other than her terrified whimpers. The sirens continue to go off and the wind picks up outside. When the lights flicker, I curse under my breath.

"What?" Rylie pulls back and stares at me with helpless, panicked eyes. Her tearstained cheeks are bright red. When the lights flicker again, she jumps. "Hudson!"

I grip her head with both hands. "Rylie. Calm down. It's just a storm. Nothing bad is going to happen."

She blinks rapidly at me, a garbled sound trapped in her throat. Thunder strikes hard and loud nearby, making us both flinch.

"It's just us," I say softly to calm her. "Playing on the sandy beach in front of our cabin. Mom and Dad are getting the burgers ready to grill. Can you play pretend with me?"

Some of the terror bleeds from her expression. "I think I heard a fish splash in the water."

"Dad will want to catch that fish," I tell her with a smile. "I found a cool rock. Same color as your hair."

"Nobody likes brown rocks," she says, her freckled nose scrunching.

I grin at her and tug at her messy hair. "But look at how pretty this brown is. It's Rylie brown. Special."

A smile breaches her face. "You think it's special?"

"Very special. I bet all the crayon companies will be beating down our door soon asking for your permission to use it in their box."

Her cheeks turn pink and she giggles. "I'd make them fight over it. It would be funny."

The wind howls and the lights flicker again, but Rylie is distracted. At least if we blow away, we'll both be smiling. Another year and I'll be gone off to college. Will she have to sit in the bathtub alone when Mom and Dad are at work?

As Rylie babbles about crayons, my future hits me hard in the chest. I'm about to go off into the world and leave my family behind. It's exciting and I'm looking forward to it, but I'll miss them. With the threat of my leaving every bit as real as the tornado warning looming over us, I feel oddly nostalgic. Like I want to hold on to this moment a little longer.

The lights flicker off for good and the howling becomes louder. Rylie is no longer distracted and buries her head against my chest. I hug her tight and kiss her hair.

"It's okay, Ry. I promise. I'll keep you safe. I won't let you down."

She clings to me for what feels like hours until her sobs and terror fade away. The storms long subside and the lights come back on, but I don't get up from the tub. And she makes no moves to get up either. I just hold her—I hold my own childhood a little while longer as my future beckons for me to grow up and become a man. Her breathing is soft and even, but she's not asleep. It's as though she knows I need this moment.

I'm lost in twisting a strand of her hair when I hear a sweet sigh.

"My babies."

I dart my eyes to the doorway. Mom stands there wearing a bright smile. She's soaked from the rain and her hair is a mess, but she's beautiful.

"Tornado sirens," I explain.

She nods and her smile fades. "A small one ripped through town. There were some uprooted trees and missing shingles near the shop. I'm just glad you're both okay."

Absently, I stroke my fingers through Rylie's hair. "Who will sit in the bathtub with her once I go to college?"

Rylie flinches in my grip and I find myself patting her back to comfort her.

"Don't worry about stuff like that, Huds. Just worry about getting yourself an education. Rylie's a big girl. She'll surprise you one day."

I wake up to the feeling of someone watching me. In the dark. It would be alarming except I know it's just Rylie.

Her fingertips are running along my scalp through my hair. Offering me the same sort of comfort I gave her. It feels good, so I can see why she likes it. I drift in and out of sleep as she touches my head. When her fingertips skate along my jaw, I'm wide awake. She runs them along my throat to my pectoral muscle through my shirt. Then, she splays her palm there. I cover her hand with mine, letting her know I'm awake and here for her.

"Do you want to talk?" I ask, my voice raspy from sleep.

"No."

I smile in the dark. Her sassy one-word answer reminds me of when we were kids. "You remember when I used to try to con you into making me food all the time?"

Her body stiffens. "It never worked."

"Sometimes it did. If I was extra nice to you," I say, amusement in my tone.

She relaxes. "You were so mean. All you had to do was say please and I would've done anything for you."

We're quiet for a moment.

"Talk to me then," I murmur. *"Please."*

"I feel so alone," she whispers, her voice barely audible.

"You're not alone, though. You have me."

She swallows and burrows against me, as though she can climb right inside me to seek shelter. "I don't, though."

"Just a few more weeks and then I'll be off for spring break. I'll come back home. Maybe we can do something fun. Go to the movies or float down the river or go camping," I tell her. "You have me. I'm right here. I've been a shitty brother, I know, but I want to try harder for you. Mom and Dad would want us to get along and lean on each other during this time."

"I want that too," she says after a few minutes.

I run my fingers back through her hair. She shivers and snuggles closer. When her leg brushes against my cock, I let out a hiss.

"Stop wiggling so much," I complain.

"Sorry."

She settles and I try to ignore the fact blood is now pumping to my dick. It reminds me I still have to tell Amy about Jada. The secret is eating me alive.

"I cheated on Amy," I admit to my sister. "A girl named Jada."

"What?"

Swallowing down the disgust at myself, I nod. "I...I...I was lonely too." It's a shitty answer, but it's the only one I've got.

"Are you going to tell her?" she asks.

"Yeah. Eventually."

"We're fucked up," she says with a small laugh.

I grin and kiss her hair. "That we are, heathen. That we are."

"She'll forgive you." Her fingers trek back up the front of my chest to my neck. "She'll probably cry a lot, though."

A groan escapes me. "Yeah."

"Do you ever wonder if she's really the one, Huds? Just because you two will have a baby doesn't mean you have to stay with her. Does she even make you happy?" Her curious fingers are back on my face and her thumb runs along my bottom lip.

"We're not having a baby." Amy must have told her because I sure as hell didn't. "It was just a scare."

"Good," she snips out. "I was worried."

I smile against her fingers that have fanned out over my lips. "What are you doing?"

"Learning who you are." Her fingers start to pull away, but I gently grip her wrist so she won't stop. If she needs this to feel better, I'll give it to her. "I spend a lot of time in the dark," she says with a whisper. "Always alone. But now you're here with me and I'm trying to understand why."

"Because you're my sister and we need each other," I tell her simply. Then I playfully bite on her fingers.

She lets out a happy squeal that I haven't heard since she was ten years old as she tugs her hand away and slaps my chest. "You bit me!" Hearing her laughter is like a shot of adrenaline to my system. Suddenly, like an addict, I want to hear it more.

I chomp the air, my teeth clanking together, enjoying her little giggles. She tries to push my face away when I start nipping the air closer and closer to her. I turn my head and bite her wrist. She tries to knee me in the balls, but I manage to pin her skinny leg between my two powerful ones. Her squirming stops and we both breathe heavily. I realize our awkward proximity and start to move away. But it's like she doesn't want to sever the link because she goes with me, her knee sliding higher. I wince, expecting my balls to get smashed, but she just rests her leg against them.

If Aunt Becky came downstairs, she'd have a fucking fit to see us like this. But it's not like that. We just need the other right now. We're not doing anything wrong. She's my sister.

"Hudson," she breathes, her hot breath tickling my neck. It reminds me of the way Amy does sometimes, which is a confusing thought. "I'm sick."

"You're not sick," I assure her. "Depression may be an illness they've labeled you with, but you're not sick. We can work through it."

"Hudson…"

I wait for her to elaborate, the air thick with her intent. She simply exhales heavily and relaxes.

"I love you."

"I love you too, heathen."

SIX

Rylie

I can make it.

Just three more days.

Hudson will be home for spring break and we can do all the things he promised me.

"Open up and show me," Aunt Becky demands, both hands on her hips as she glares at me.

"Ahhhh," I say, sticking my tongue out, and then roll my eyes.

"Good, now get ready for school."

She leaves me alone in the bathroom. I used to love my aunt, but now I can't stand her. It's like she thrives on controlling my every move. You'd think I would have some freedom, but ever since the day I took all my medication and landed myself in the hospital, I have none. She watches my every move. Dictates my every action. Tells me when I can breathe.

I close the door behind her and turn on the shower. As I undress, I stare at my body, unimpressed. I'm nearly a woman stuck in a child's body. My breasts are barely B cups. You can see my rib bones and hip bones protruding. I'm not at all curvy like Amy.

Irritation flitters through me.

Amy weighs my brother down.

He deserves better.

Like you?

A shiver trembles down my spine. I seek out the warmth and privacy the shower will offer. No locks. No medicine. No sharp things. Dr. Livingston and Aunt Becky make sure I'm not a harm to myself. My legs are prickly as are my underarms. I wish badly to shave, but I've been grounded from that too.

With a heavy sigh, I wash my body in the fancy shower. Sometimes it feels like I'm staying in a swanky hotel. It's so different here than where I lived with my family. Nicer and more expensive. But certainly not home. I close my eyes and try to recall the nights I spent curled up against Hudson in the basement before he left to go back to Arkansas. After that first night, it was like I needed him to breathe. I'd expected him to go back to his usual jerky ways, but he held me each night.

It was driving me to insanity.

What he sees as innocent cuddling with his sister is something completely different to me. I tried to warn him I was sick, but he shooed my comment away. He doesn't understand. And clearly doesn't feel the same way. But because of my sickness, I can't push him away and find someone or something else to focus on.

Just him.

I reach up and grab the removable showerhead. It's dirty and wrong, but I think of *him* touching me between my thighs. The hot water blasts my clit and I gasp. Desperate to feel more of the pleasure, I pull apart my pussy lips and assault my sensitive flesh with the water. It feels good, but what makes it feel better is pretending it's *his* tongue. Licking me. Hot and wet. Never stopping.

Sick, sick, sick, Rylie.

Yet, I don't stop.

I imagine things no girl should think of when she pleasures herself. Thoughts that could lead to actions with awful consequences. When I think of *his* teeth biting my fingers, I orgasm. Hard, violent, unapologetic.

I just had an orgasm to thoughts of my brother.

Shame slides through me like oil spreading on a lake. It's dirty and coats every part of me inside and out. Black and wrong.

I can't do that again.

My clit throbs in response.

Maybe just once more…

⸚

Me: Did you listen to that song I sent?

Hudson: You sent me like ten. Which one?

Me: All of them, nerd.

Hudson: I like the third one.

I smile as I read his text. The third one was my favorite too.

Hudson: How are you? You haven't had any more of those thoughts, have you?

Heat flushes across my skin.

Me: What?

How does he know?

Hudson: Hurting yourself, Ry. You haven't thought about it anymore, have you?

I let out a ragged breath of realization. Those thoughts. Not the shameful ones. Got it.

Me: No. Not really.

My phone starts ringing and I hurry to answer it. If Aunt

Becky knew I was staying up until two in the morning texting, she'd take my phone away. Again. It took apologizing and helping Aunt Becky pull weeds to make up for smashing her mirror, but I eventually got my phone replaced and privileges back.

"What?" I whisper.

Hudson chuckles. Deep and throaty. It vibrates straight to my core. If I said I only touched myself twice that day in the shower, I'd be a liar. I've touched myself every time in the shower since.

"Most people say hello when they answer the phone," he says, amusement in his tone.

"I'm not like most people."

His laughter dies and he grows serious. "Rylie, what does that mean? 'Not really?'"

My heart rate picks up at his concern. "I just meant that yes, I get sad a lot, but talking to you helps."

He lets out a heavy breath. "Don't ever say shit like that to me again." He pauses for a moment. "I was so fucking scared when I got the call from Aunt Becky. I thought I lost you too," he murmurs.

"I'm sorry," I whisper. "I really am."

"You should be in bed," he grumbles.

"I *am* in bed."

"Smartass."

I slide my hand under the blanket and delve into my panties. My fingers lightly brush against my clit as I try to steady my breathing. "Will the hurt ever go away?"

"I hope so."

We're both quiet for a moment.

"I miss you," I whine, tears threatening. I'm overwhelmed by thoughts and sensations. I want to cry and crawl into his lap. I want to touch myself and think of him. I want to scream and destroy my room. I want it all. All at once. It's maddening as I try to sort it all out in my head.

"I'll see you tomorrow," he promises. "You should get some sleep."

Lazily, I rub myself between my thighs, enjoying the sparks of pleasure that buzz through me. It feels forbidden to touch myself while talking to him. "Did you tell Amy yet?"

"No."

"When are you going to tell her?"

"Probably on my break," he says with a heavy sigh.

"Did you see Jada anymore?"

"I've seen her, but we haven't messed around."

"Did you kiss her?"

He swallows audibly. "Yeah, once before. But what was so bad was I let her blow me."

I close my eyes as I envision some beautiful woman on her knees in front of Hudson. Did he fist her hair? Did she swallow his cum? "You didn't have sex with her?"

"No," he growls.

I rub my clit faster and faster, growing dizzy by how good it feels and how it's heightened by being on the phone with him.

"Rylie." His voice is sharp and commanding. It sends me over the edge. I bite on my bottom lip to keep from crying out. My breathing is heavy, but I get it to calm down before I answer him.

"Y-Yes?"

"Go to sleep, heathen."

I'm happy.

Really happy.

The sensation is a foreign one, but I clutch onto it desperately.

Hudson will be here soon. I've missed him like crazy. As soon as I hear his car door slam out front, I take off out the door. I run straight for him and throw myself into his arms. He chuckles when I nearly knock him over. My legs are latched at his waist and my arms around his neck.

God, he smells so good.

"I missed you," I murmur against his neck.

"Hey, Rylie," Amy says from nearby.

Embarrassed to have an audience, I slide down his body to my feet. When I glance over at her, she's smiling at me with the fakest smile ever.

"I didn't expect to see you here," I bite out as I pull away from my brother.

"Don't be a brat," Hudson teases and playfully tugs at a strand of my hair. "Amy and I picked up food and some Redbox movies. Thought we could get the week started. I did promise you movies." He grins at me. Wide and adorable and boyish.

I don't have the heart to tell him I don't want to do anything with her.

I thought it would just be us.

"Okay," I say, forcing a smile.

He frowns at me but doesn't press. We go inside and I try to ignore Aunt Becky and Uncle Randy while they fuss over how wonderful and beautiful Amy is and how much they've missed seeing her. I grab the movies and head downstairs. Tears threaten, but I keep them at bay. I'm stupid. Delusional even. Did I really think I could spend an entire week flirting with my brother?

Sick. Sick. Sick. Sick.

What's wrong with me?

"Rylie…"

His voice startles me and I jump. I can't even look at him. What if he sees the sickness inside me? Will he be disgusted?

"Rylie," he says again, this time closer.

When his strong arms wrap around me from behind, I burst into tears. I can't help it. I'm frustrated and confused and upset.

"Hey now," he says, his voice soft and comforting. He twists me around until I'm facing him. "I didn't realize how upset you were."

I cry against his shirt, wishing the entire world around us would disappear. That we could turn off the lights and sleep side by side on the couch like we'd done in the past. In the dark. Just him and me.

"I'm sorry," he whispers against my hair. "I didn't know."

Didn't know what?

That I'm completely obsessed with him?

The thought only makes me cry harder.

"Hey, guys," Amy chirps from the stairs. "Everything okay?"

Reluctantly, I start to pull away.

"Can you give us a few more minutes alone?" he asks, hugging me back to him.

"Sure," she squeaks out. "Of course." Her footsteps retreat and the door closes behind her.

Hudson doesn't rush me to calm down. He simply strokes my hair and kisses the top of my head. It soothes my broken heart and empty soul.

Time passes slowly, but it comforts me knowing it passes with him.

Amy's voice is once again getting under my skin.

"It's been over an hour. Should I ask Becky to take me home?"

"Yes," Hudson says at the same time I say, "No."

I tilt my head up to look at him. His nose is red and I wonder if he was crying too. He clenches his jaw and pierces me with an intense stare.

"Are you sure?" he asks me.

"Yeah, let's watch a movie."

SEVEN

Hudson

I knew this was a bad idea.

Rylie is too fragile. Aunt Becky gives me the updates when I'm not talking to Rylie herself. If it weren't for Amy blowing up my goddamned phone and guilting me into seeing her, I would've gone straight here. Now, I wish I'd manned up and told her I'd see her a different day.

Amy flashes me a worried look, but I simply shake my head at her. It's too late now. We'll get through tonight. Then, I'll make it up to her.

To Rylie.

I owe it to her.

"We picked out a funny movie," Amy says with false cheer.

"Okay," Rylie says as she curls up on one end of the sofa. Retreating. I see it in her eyes. It makes me want to grab her and pull her outside of her own head.

"Great," Amy chirps. She hands me the movie and plants herself in the middle of the sofa. Irritation blossoms inside me. I'm being unfair by being annoyed with Amy, but I can't help it. It's like she's trying to make things harder.

I get the movie started and then sit on the opposite end as Rylie. Amy practically climbs into my lap. The movie starts and soon Amy is laughing at every scene.

Rylie stares at the screen, lost in her mind.

I clench my teeth, desperate to push Amy away and pull my sister to me. To ask her what has her so upset and how I can fix it. Rylie must sense me staring at her because she turns my way. Her stare skims over Amy and then she regards me with watery eyes.

"Are you okay?" I mouth to her.

She nods and turns back to the television. From my vantage point, I don't miss the tear that streaks down her cheek or the hasty way she swipes it away. By the time the movie ends, I'm practically jumping off the couch to take Amy home.

"Let's go. It's getting late and I'm tired," I say rather sharply.

Amy frowns at me but nods. "Y-Yeah, of course."

"I'll be back soon," I tell Rylie. She tries to smile but even that fails. When I walk past her, I ruffle her hair. "I'll be back soon. I promise."

The drive back to Amy's house where she lives with her parents is quiet. It isn't until I'm sitting in her driveway with the car in park that she speaks.

"Is everything okay with you, Hudson?" She pauses for a minute. "With us?"

"Of course it is. I just have a lot on my mind." Understatement of the year.

Her lip trembles. "You feel so distant lately. Like I'm a bother to be around."

I take her hand, but my tone is sharp. "I lost both my parents and my sister is severely depressed. My focus is elsewhere."

She winces as though I've struck her. "I know. I'm sorry. When you put it that way, I feel selfish."

"I just need time to make sure my sister is okay," I utter

and scrub my palm down the side of my face. "Can you give me that?"

She nods and leans forward to kiss me. I offer her my cheek and pat her hand.

"I'll call you tomorrow," I tell her as she pulls away.

"I love you," she says tearfully.

"I love you too."

She climbs out of the car and I wait to make sure she gets in okay. My thoughts are a mess, though.

"I love you."

"I love you too."

But do I?

I cheated on her, for fuck's sake.

My relationship with Amy needs to take a back seat. I can ponder on all of it when Rylie is more stable. Right now, she's my focus. Ry is the only thing I have left.

When I get back, the house is dark. Rylie isn't in the basement, so I go upstairs looking for her. The light under the bathroom door shines out into the dark hallway, indicating she's inside. I'm just about to knock and ask if she's okay when the door opens. With big, sad brown eyes, she stares up at me. Her face is free of makeup. All her freckles are on full display.

"Are you okay?" My voice is husky and raw with emotion. She looks so fucking broken right now.

Water drips from her hair and skates down bare shoulders. It's then I realize she's just wearing a towel. Her collarbone protrudes and she's so pale.

"Have you not been eating?" I demand, motioning at

her body.

She glances past me down the hallway. Right. Aunt Becky. The last thing I need is for her to come join an argument about my sister's weight. She's vulnerable enough as it is. I grip her wrist and urge her back into the bathroom, closing the door behind me.

"Rylie," I growl. "Talk to me, dammit."

Her dark brows furl together. "I'm never hungry."

I clench my jaw. "You still have to eat."

She shrugs and it pisses me off.

"Rylie, you still have to eat."

Her nostrils flare and she gives me a small shove. "Lower your voice. Aunt Becky will be in here forcing food down my throat and God knows what other kind of medicine."

"Come here," I grumble, opening my arms.

She steps into my hug and her body relaxes. In her towel, it's easier to notice how bony she is. It fucking worries me to death.

"I'm going to dry my hair and then go to bed," she murmurs.

Disappointment floods through me. Where's the girl from last night? The one who chatted about bands and music?

I pull away and grip her cold biceps. "If you need me, you know where I'll be."

She doesn't answer but pulls away. I let out a heavy sigh and leave her be. After a quick shower downstairs in the basement, I pull on some basketball shorts and flick off the lights. I lie down on the couch and stare up at the ceiling in the darkness. The basement has no windows, which is nice when you want to sleep in but right now, I feel trapped. Closed in. Hopeless.

"I can't sleep," a soft voice whispers.

"Me neither."

I don't have to tell her to come because she's already crawling on top of me, seeking my comfort. I drag the blanket over us and stroke her still warm now dry hair. I'm hyperaware that I'm only wearing a pair of shorts. Whatever she's wearing feels thin. A pair of sleep shorts and a tank top maybe. Through her clothes, her bony ribs dig into me as she situates herself. My heart aches.

"Is this normal?" she asks, her voice barely audible.

"What?"

Her palm slides up my bare chest and her fingers flit along my jaw. Then, her thumb rubs across my bottom lip.

"I don't know," I lie. It's far from normal. I'm pretty sure if Amy or Aunt Becky saw the way we've been cuddling at night, they might have something to say about it.

But why?

We're not doing anything wrong.

Right?

"Normal is overrated," she murmurs, her hot breath tickling my chest.

I run my fingertips down her spine over her shirt and then settle my palm on her lower back. Her breathing evens out and soon she's drooling on my chest as she sleeps. I slide my fingers up and down her back. I'm not sure if I'm soothing her or if it's soothing me to do this. Either way, I like it. I feel calm for the first time since I've been back home for break.

She's my sister.

We lost our parents.

This may not be normal to most people, but it's normal for us.

I wake up sweating. Tangled up with another person. I'm smashing her into the cushions with my weight. I fumble in the darkness, seeking her hip to move her from the crack of the couch. Instead of finding hip, I find bare skin over her ribs. It's shocking they're so defined. I rub my fingers along each one, dipping into the grooves between them until my thumb brushes along something fleshy and soft. It takes a second to realize I just touched my sister's breast. By accident and the underside, but I still touched it.

Fuck.

"I'm just not hungry," she murmurs the moment I slide my thumb back down over her ribs.

I freeze, wondering if she'll call me a sicko for touching her. I should apologize, but shame has my lips remaining glued shut. I turn toward her face and my nose brushes against her cheek.

"I wish you'd try and eat," I say finally.

"I'll try."

Lately, my life feels so fucked up, but in the dark, it feels okay. With Rylie safe and cared for, I feel relaxed and not so goddamned stressed.

"When you graduate, can I live with you?" she asks, her hot breath tickling my face.

"Yes," I say without hesitation. Amy will just have to get over it. If that's what Rylie needs to thrive, then so be it.

"I still won't make you food," she teases.

My heart clenches in my chest. It's the first sign of happiness in my sister I've seen all night. "I'll just have to find something to eat," I say, clacking my teeth as though I'm seeking out something to eat on her.

"Hudson," she hisses, laughter in her voice.

I playfully bite her. Her jaw it would seem. We both freeze.

"I'm sick," she whimpers. Another reminder.

"Maybe I'm sick too." I press a kiss to the place I just bit her.

She lets out a groan and her fingers rake down the side of my arm. I kiss her jaw again. Or is it her neck?

"I like it when you laugh," I whisper, my lips dusting over her flesh. "I like it when you eat." I clutch her bare ribs again. "I like it when you're happy."

Nothing makes sense right now.

In an effort to comfort Rylie, I've lost sight of who we are.

The darkness hides us.

For a minute, we're free.

Her thigh slides over my hip. Dirty thoughts run rampant in my mind. Maybe I should have fucked Amy to clear my head because right now, my thoughts are not where they should be.

"Rylie," I groan, my lips hovering over her neck. "I don't think this is normal."

"I like how this makes me feel."

Digging deep for some shred of self-control, I pry my lips away from her neck and slide my palm away from her bare flesh. It had been inching up and I was going to do something more than an accidental touching. That's the last thing I need to do. Fuck my sister up even more.

"Maybe you should sleep in your bed," I grumble, hating the words as they leave my mouth.

"Please don't make me leave." Her voice cracks at the end.

Hauling her closer, I hug her tight. "Never. Just go to sleep. Otherwise…" My words hang heavy in the air. "Just go to sleep."

"I'll try."

"I'll try too."

"Hudson?"

"Yeah?"

"Please don't be weird about this tomorrow."

I smile and kiss her hair. "I'll try."

"I'll try too."

EIGHT

Rylie

"Camping. I don't know..." Aunt Becky trails off.

I know she's torn between controlling me and getting me out of her hair. She and Randy could never have kids. I think almost two months of having me live here, she realizes she dodged a bullet. I'm not easy by any means.

"I'll make her take her medicine," Hudson assures her.

I blush when he winks at me. This morning, I slipped out of the basement and snuck into the shower because I needed relief. After last night, my mind has been buzzing like mad.

My brother.

I can't make sense of it.

Last night was...nice.

The way he touched me felt so intimate. Like a spell I didn't want to break. In the dark, it's easy to be brave. In the bright light of the day, I melt under his intense stares.

"Fine. Be careful. No drinking, Huds. If you guys float down the river, be careful. I don't want a call saying my niece and nephew drowned in the Niangua." She purses her lips and then waves us along. "You're burning daylight. Go."

A couple of hours later and we're in the car headed to the river. It's nearly a two-hour drive and we should arrive later this afternoon with plenty of time to enjoy the sunshine. Hudson turns on a playlist of the songs I've been sending him. I'm overly giddy of the fact he's taken the time to collect the songs. We listen to Radiohead and I Google campsites. Hudson tells me about his friend Nick and some of the other baseball players. But mostly, we talk about Mom and Dad. It's therapeutic. I don't like talking to Aunt Becky even though Mom was her older sister. I'm not sure Hudson talks to Amy about them much either. It's like something we can bond over. Our loss. Our memories. Our family.

"Did Amy not want to come with us?" I ask, my eyes on him.

His Aviators hide his eyes, but I can tell he's tense about the question. "She wasn't invited."

"Oh."

He reaches forward and turns down the music. "I told her I wanted to focus on you. We've been through some shit, Ry. I just think we deserve this time to work through things."

Emotion clogs my throat. All I can do is nod. "Thank you for doing this."

He flashes me a brilliant smile that makes my heart rate pick up. "We're going to have fun."

Happiness blooms inside of me like a sweet-smelling rose. I admire this new bloom as we cruise the road singing along to songs. Two hours pass quickly and soon we're loading our gear into a raft. I wanted a canoe because they look badass, but Hudson asked me to trust him.

And since I do, I agreed to do the raft instead.

After watching three different couples capsize in their canoes while we cruise on past, I'm glad I listened. Hudson and I have been able to just sit back and enjoy the ride.

"It's hot today," I complain, but I refuse to take off my tank top. Now that Hudson has pointed out how skinny he thinks I am, I'm self-conscious to be seen in a swimsuit.

"Here, let me help you cool off." He smirks before leaning over the side and scooping up cold river water into his hand. I scream when he hurtles a whole handful at me, soaking my shirt. Yanking off my sunglasses, I swipe at the water on my face with the back of my hand.

"Asshole," I bite out.

He laughs and then sits up before peeling off his T-shirt. I quickly put my sunglasses back on so I don't get caught appreciating his physique. Baseball has been good to him. He plays third base and his shoulders are broad. His biceps are large and defined. And abs. Hudson has countable abs. Unaware of my staring, he sits up on his knees and uses the paddle to guide us over to a sandy bank. His ass is defined too and his navy-blue trunks hang low enough that I can see a sliver of his ass crack. When we near the beachy area, he climbs out and splashes into the water before dragging the raft with me and all our gear in it onto the beach as if it weighs nothing.

"We can rest here and eat. And swim since you're so hot," he teases. He places his hands on his tapered hips and stares downstream. I sneak in a peek at his V. The trail of hair from his belly button that disappears into his trunks is fascinating and beautiful. The outline of is cock is thick and proud in his trunks. It's not erect, but it's big.

"Swim first or eat first?" His jaw clenches and I know I've been caught staring.

Heat floods through me, making me blush. "Swim." I definitely need to cool off because I'm pretty sure I'm drooling.

Sick. Sick. Sick. Sick.

He saunters past me, tossing his glasses into the raft, and wades out into the river. Then, he turns and stares back at me, his glittering green eyes on full display. "Well, what are you waiting for?"

To grow boobs and hips and thighs.

"Don't watch me," I grumble.

He laughs but turns away. I quickly peel off my tank and shorts, leaving me in a simple orange bikini. I lose my sunglasses too and head his way. With my arms covering as much as I can, I run past him into the icy water. I screech and stop when I'm waist deep.

"It's too cold!" I cry out. "Why are we here?"

"You have to get your whole body wet. You'll get used to it."

"Fuck no," I argue, but it's too late. His strong arm sweeps around my waist and he carries me deep. It's so cold. "Asshole!"

Then he plunges us under the surface. I thrash to the top and sputter out a bunch of curse words. He flicks his head, sending his brown hair whipping back, and he grins at me. Cute and boyish and sweet. Not at all like a person who just tried to drown me.

"Careful," he warns. "Don't go out too far. The current is strong." He grabs my wrist and pulls me until we can both touch the rocky bottom. His other hand grips my waist when I wobble, but he doesn't let go. Not that I want him to. The heat from his fingers warms me.

"How's baseball?" I ask, leaning closer to him.

He lets out a heavy sigh. "Coach Brass has given me lots of time to get my head on straight, but I think his patience is wearing thin. I struck out twice last game." His brows pull into a frown. "Without Mom and Dad coming to the games, I don't...I just don't enjoy it much."

"Mom would be so proud," I murmur.

His nostrils flare and he looks away. "No, she'd tell me to get my head out of my ass and hit the damn ball."

We both laugh because it's true.

"And Dad would say, 'Now, Lauren, he's doing the best he can. Give the kid a break.'" Thoughts of my dad trying to calm my mom down flood through me and suddenly nothing is funny. A whine climbs up my throat.

"Shh," Hudson murmurs as he pulls me against his chest.

He holds me tight as I soak his chest with tears.

"I miss them."

"Me too."

His palms rub my back in a comforting way. I'm immediately distracted from my emotions over my parents because my brother's big, strong hands feel good against my bare skin.

"Come on," he says, his voice husky. "Let's get something to eat."

I follow him out of the water and watch him efficiently lay out a blanket on the sand. Then, he digs around in the ice chest. He tosses me a bottle of water. I down half the bottle before closing it and sitting on the blanket. Lying back, I shield the sun with my arm and close my eyes.

"You need to eat something." He sits beside me and water from his body drips onto mine.

"Later."

He taps a grape to my lips. "Nope. Now."

I accept the grape and find myself wanting another one. One by one, he alternates feeding us grapes. When he's satisfied we've had enough, he gets up and stuffs them back in the ice chest.

"You're burning."

Tell me about it.

"I'm fine," I murmur.

Something cold squirts across my abdomen and I squeal.

He grins at me. "You need sunscreen." His smile falls as he begins rubbing in the sunscreen on my stomach.

"Hudson…"

"Yeah?"

"Thank you."

His palm rubs rigorously all over my stomach until he's smeared it in. Twice his hand sweeps across my lower stomach and I let out a small moan. Thank God he ignores the embarrassing sounds coming from me. He continues his task and squirts more sunscreen out, this time into his hand. My shoulders get attention next. Then my neck. My collarbone.

"Will you do my back too?" I ask, desperate to have him keep touching me.

"Roll over."

I lie down face first and squeal again when he squirts it on my back. But then his warm, powerful hands are spreading it around my back. His fingers dip along my sides and I shiver.

"This is in the way," he tells me, his voice low, a near whisper.

He plucks the strings tied at the middle of my back and pulls them away. Then, he rubs me lazily and slowly. I'm sure the sunscreen is more than smeared in, but he doesn't stop rubbing my back.

"This feels good," I murmur.

"I know."

"Want me to put some on you?" I ask.

He runs his fingertips down my spine. "I do."

"Do you want to fix my swimsuit?"

A pause.

"Yeah."

He ties it back and when I sit up on my knees to look at him, he has his back to me. I pick up the bottle of sunscreen and pour some into my hands. Running my hands over his muscled shoulders, I take my time rubbing it in. At first, he's tense, but then he relaxes. We're silent as I move around to his front. His legs are stretched out in front of him. Boldly, I straddle his thighs, facing him. Neither of us speaks or looks at the other. It's as if we're collectively holding our breaths. I focus on getting the sunscreen on him. His breath hitches when my fingers brush low on his stomach. Between us, I can tell he's getting hard. I don't want him to freak out and kill the moment, so I try to distract him.

"What will we do later this week?" I ask, chancing a glance at his face.

His jaw is clenched as his intense green eyes bore into mine. "What do you want to do?"

"I want to see Mom and Dad's gravesite."

"Of course," he rumbles. His eyes drop to my lips and then he looks away. "We should get going. I want to find a better place to camp."

As if I weigh nothing, he grips my hips and moves me out of his lap. My heart sinks until I notice his erection tenting his trunks that he's trying desperately to hide from me.

Maybe it's true.

Maybe he's sick too.

NINE

Hudson

I'm losing my mind.

Quickly.

I feel like somewhere since my parents' deaths, we crossed a line. We crossed a line that normal brothers and sisters don't cross. A line we somehow skated over without realizing it.

Fuck.

I don't know what to do. My mind reels and yet I can't keep my eyes off her. Each laugh has me held hostage. Each smile I'm caught staring.

"There?" she asks, pointing to where some people are camping.

I'd rather not, but we're running out of options. It's getting dark and being on the river at night isn't safe.

"Hey!" a man with a giant belly and big gray beard calls out. "Y'all can camp here. We don't bite."

A woman with an equally big pot belly laughs. "Speak for yourself, Danny."

Rylie laughs at them and it makes the decision for me. We'll camp with these old people. I hop out and Danny waddles into the water to help me. Together, we pull the raft on the banks.

"I'm Danny Franklin and this is my wife, Joya."

"You kids got here just in time. Supper is on the fire,"

she says, smiling. She's missing her front tooth, but she has kind eyes.

"Something hot sure beats the cold sandwiches in our ice chest," I say with a grin. "I'm Hudson and this is my—"

"Your girlfriend is shy," Danny interrupts, a wide grin on his face. "I'm like Santa, baby girl. Once you get to know me, you want to sit on my lap."

Neither Ry nor I correct him.

Joya snorts and slaps his arm. "You'll scare these kids away. Hudson, ignore him. Sweetheart?"

"Rylie," she answers. "Thank you for inviting us."

Rylie comes to stand by my side. She's nervous. I wrap an arm around her and pull her to me.

"Why don't you go help Joya and I'll work on getting our camp set up?"

She nods and follows after Joya over to the fire. Danny winks at me.

"Joya was sixteen when we met. I put three babies in her before she turned twenty-one," he boasts. "Your girl is young, eh?"

"She'll be eighteen in April."

He nods. "I'm not the law. Your secret is safe with me."

I should tell him she's my sister, but there's something forbidden and alluring to pretending she's not. "Thanks."

He whistles and chatters as we erect my small tent. It's meant for one, but Rylie's small and likes to cuddle anyway.

"I snore," he warns. "So don't worry about making noise." He waggles his brows.

Laughing, I clasp my hand over his shoulder. "We'll be quiet."

As the sun disappears completely, the temperature drops. Rylie stands by the fire, shivering as she eats a hot dog. I down mine quickly and locate the blanket from our tent. When I come back, I sit in the sand and motion for Rylie to sit with me. She scurries over to me and sits between my spread legs. I wrap the blanket around us and warm her up.

She turns her head and whispers, "They think we're boyfriend and girlfriend."

Nuzzling my nose against her hair that smells like sunshine, river water, and sunscreen, I inhale her. "They do."

"You didn't correct them."

"Neither did you."

My palm slides down her arm and I link my fingers with hers. "It's none of their business either way."

"Look at them whispering," Joya says and slaps Danny's arm. "Remember when we were young and adorable like that?"

"Now we're old and adorable," Danny explains with a chuckle.

I'm content to hold Rylie. I love the way her body shakes when she giggles at their banter. The lines are definitely blurred because for a moment, I delude myself into thinking we're actually a couple. Right here on the sandy banks of the river, we're not brother and sister. I'm not in a committed relationship with Amy Kent. We're just two people. Two people who like to touch.

Danny and Joya jabber on until I find my head nodding. Rylie has fallen asleep. I thank them for the food and then wake her. The air is nippy, so we hurry to our tent. It's a tight squeeze, but we eventually zip ourselves in and cuddle under the blanket. We're both sticky and smelly, but it doesn't stop us from clinging to the other.

"Hudson?"

"Yeah, Ry?"

"Today was fun." Her palm splays out over my bare chest. "I can't remember the last time I had fun."

"Hmm," I say, smiling. "Your birthday?"

She snorts. "It rained on the barbeque. That was not fun."

"But the mud fight Dad started was," I argue.

Her body tenses and I hold her tighter. "It was fun, Ry."

"It was." She sniffles. "Christmas was not fun."

My stomach feels hollow at her words. Christmas was not fun. I was an asshole to her. Mom was fussing over her and I got pissed. There I was, barely back from being away at school, and Rylie was once again making things difficult.

But looking back, I saw the unmasked pain in her eyes. I was too selfish to want to help like Mom and Dad did. All I cared about was myself. And getting between Amy's legs.

"Why were you so upset that night?" I ask, my voice gruff. She knows which night. The night I ended up yelling at my mom to stop enabling her and stormed off. I spent the night with Amy and didn't come home until dinner the next day.

She stiffens and lets out a sad sigh. "Because I missed you. When you're not home, it's lonely. It's like you fill the space with life. You were home and then you were making plans to go see Amy. I don't know how to explain it. I was just upset."

"I'm here now," I mutter. "I'm sorry, Rylie. I'm sorry I've been an awful brother."

"You keep telling me that, but, see, I didn't see it that way. I just wanted to spend time with you."

The tent is cramped, but I need to comfort her. I roll us until she's mostly beneath me. My bare leg intertwines with hers beneath the blanket and my palm slides up her stomach over her tank.

"I'm trying to be a better person," I admit. I brush her hair from her face and touch her lips with my fingertips.

"You were always a better person than me. I worshipped you," she breathes.

"And now?" My voice is husky.

"I still do."

"What's happening to us?" I rest my head on my arm as I pet her hair with my other hand. "Why do I feel so desperate to fix our relationship?"

She turns her head, her hot breath tickling my face. "Because I'm all you have left."

Leaning forward, I plant a kiss on her cheek. "It's more than that. I think with Mom and Dad passing, my eyes are finally open to what's important. All the shit I worried about before doesn't matter anymore."

"I'm glad you're back this week," she murmurs. "I'll be sad when you leave."

I kiss her cheek again. Just a small peck. And then she tilts her head toward me. I can feel her breath so close. I press my lips to hers because it feels right.

"Hudson?"

"Yeah, Rylie?"

"I'm sick and you've caught the sickness too."

I peck her lips once more before lying back. "I'll be fine, Ry. Don't worry about me."

She curls back against me and whispers against my chest, "I'm worried it's going to kill *me*, though."

"Oh, shit," I grumble when we pull into the driveway at Aunt Becky's. "I forgot to make you take your pill."

Rylie shrugs. "I don't need it."

"You do." I reach behind her seat and dig it out of my backpack. "Here."

She lets out a huff but steals my Mountain Dew to chase down her pill. "Ahhh. There. Happy?"

I grab her hand and squeeze it. "I just don't want you to hurt. Those pills help you."

The tension bleeds from her and she nods. "I know. I'm sorry. I've just been under Aunt Becky's thumb for too long. She makes me feel like I'm in the nuthouse and she's my evil nurse."

We both laugh because Aunt Becky is kind of a control freak.

My phone rings and I groan. I've been avoiding Amy's calls. Unfairly so. She's my girlfriend and I can't avoid her forever.

"Grab a shower," I tease. "You stink. I'll unload all this."

As soon as she climbs out, I call Amy back.

"Hey, Hudson," she greets.

"Hey, babe."

"They're having a block party at the downtown district tonight. You should come. I'll be helping Mom run the store, but she'll let me out early and maybe we can watch the bands or something."

"Yeah, of course."

"I've missed you. I thought…"

"What?"

"I thought you could come alone," she murmurs, shame in her voice.

Anger swells up inside me. Of course she should feel

ashamed. She's asking me to leave behind my sister knowing she's fragile lately.

Amy bursts into tears and speaks before I can answer. "I'm sorry. Gah, I'm sorry. I shouldn't have said that. I'm just missing you and want to spend time with you."

I relax and run my fingers through my dirty hair. "I'll be there. See you soon."

"I love you," she says.

"You too."

I click off my phone and spend the next half hour unloading the truck. My mind is elsewhere as I shower and get ready. When I finally emerge from the bathroom, Rylie is passed out on the couch. She's wearing a pair of my Razorback sweats and a tank top. Her hair is pulled back in a ponytail, still wet, and her nose and cheeks are red from sunburn.

I should let her sleep.

Slip away to avoid hurting her feelings.

But…

I tickle her bare foot until her eyes flutter open.

"Amy wants us to come to a block party," I lie. "You could get away from Aunt Becky."

She sits up and yawns before standing. "You don't have to ask me twice. I'll be ready in twenty minutes." She bounds up the stairs, full of energy for someone who was just sleeping.

I'm doing the right thing.

⁓

"And we got these in yesterday," Amy chirps as she shows me some new candles.

I don't fucking care about candles, but I force a smile anyway.

"Nice."

A customer asks Amy a question about the candles and she starts animatedly telling them all about them. I sneak away on a hunt for Rylie. She leans against a wall staring at the ground, looking sorely out of place. My eyes rake over her appearance and I wonder when she grew up. She's wearing a navy-blue floral print dress, a denim jacket, and cowgirl boots. It looks like something Aunt Becky bought for her and I'm happy she's at least trying to make our aunt happy.

Her hair has been twisted into a messy bun and tendrils frame her face. She took the time to put on some mascara and lipstick, but the red on her cheeks is natural from the sun. It strikes me that she's really pretty. Too pretty.

Jerking my head around, I wonder if others see it too. A guy close to her age standing with another guy keeps flickering his eyes over to her. A surge of annoyance rises up inside of me.

"Let's take a walk. She's going to be here for a while," I say to Rylie.

She lifts her gaze and regards me with a warm smile. "I'd like to get out of here."

Side by side, we walk past the boy with the wandering eyes and I glower at him until he looks away. Once outside in the warm evening air, I sling my arm over Rylie's shoulder and walk her along the sidewalk. She leans into me as we walk, her arm hugging me at my waist.

"Chocolate?" I ask, pointing at the chocolatier store.

"How about Dizzy Dunlap's?"

The store sticks out like a sore thumb. A strobe light

flickers from inside the window. The scent of incense is strong as we walk through the doorway. The place is crowded and dark and loud. A Jimi Hendrix song plays on the speakers.

"This place is insane," I say, leaning into her ear.

She looks at me and grins, the black light making her teeth look whiter and her skin darker. Her hand wraps around mine and she drags me deeper into the store. I let her guide me until we're in a room that has people sitting on couches and mismatched chairs. Just as a couple vacates an oversized chair, we steal it. I fall into the chair and she sits on the arm. In the dark corner of the room, I let my gaze roam up her tanned-looking thigh. She props her ankles up on the other arm so her legs are stretched across me.

"What do you want for your birthday next month?" I ask, having to yell over the loud music.

"A tattoo."

I raise my brows. "A tattoo? Where?"

"Here," she says and runs her finger along her ribs.

"Mom would shit."

She shrugs. "Mom isn't here."

We're both quiet for a moment.

"I'll take you. It can be my present to you," I tell her, my voice gruff.

She leans forward and hugs my neck. "Thanks, bro."

When she pulls away, my eyes once again travel to her slender legs. I slide my knuckle along the underside of her calf. The hairs on her leg are prickly.

"You forgot to shave," I tease.

Her smile falls and she stares at me as though I've struck her. "You don't have to be an asshole." She starts to get up, but I grip her wrist just as she's standing.

"What's wrong?"

Her bright white eyes under the black light shimmer with tears. "I can't shave."

"Why not?"

"Because Aunt Becky won't let me!"

She tries to jerk away from me, but I'm stronger. I tug her into my lap and hug her to me. At first she's stiff, but then she relaxes. Her body curls into mine and her tears soak my shirt.

"Shhh," I murmur as I stroke her back over her denim jacket.

"She's afraid I'll cut myself."

TEN

Rylie

His fingers rubbing up and down my spine stop their ministrations. "She's just trying to protect you," he says, his voice gruff.

"I don't need protecting." I start to get up again, but his palm grips my bare thigh, stopping me. Heat floods through me. I should move his hand, but I find my body turning to jello at his touch.

"Yes, you do." His fingers rub along my skin in a comforting way.

I shiver. "I don't. I'm not going to cut my wrists with a shaving razor. Do you know how embarrassing it is being told you can't shave your own body when you're almost eighteen years old?"

His brows furl together. "I'll do it for you."

I blink at him. "You'll shave my legs?"

"And under your arms."

Images of him in the shower with me, shaving my legs while I hold the removable showerhead between my thighs flood through my mind, causing my flesh to heat.

"You're blushing," he teases, his palm never leaving my thigh.

Because I'm sick.

Because I want you in ways I shouldn't.

"I am not."

Under the black light, his eyes seem wild and untamed. Dangerous even. I like seeing him like this. Daring and carefree.

"There you are!"

Amy's voice has me jerking out of Hudson's lap and straightening my dress. He jumps to his feet and shoots me an intense look before accepting her hug. She looks past him at me, jealousy flaring in her eyes. The jealousy is much brighter and obvious in this place.

I want to remind her he's my brother.

That she can't be jealous of our relationship because we're family.

"Come on, guys. The band I wanted you to see is about to start," Amy chirps. She tugs at Hudson's hand and pulls him away from me.

All I can do is follow.

Alone.

We exit the hazy store and Amy babbles to people along the way that she knows. They meet up with a group of kids they went to high school with. I recognize a few faces, siblings of the older kids. Nobody I talk to. The group migrates past herds of people to a stage that's been set up in the middle of the street.

My mouth waters when I get a whiff of turkey legs being cooked by a vendor parked nearby. I want to ask Hudson if he wants to share one like when we were kids, but he's in a heated conversation with some guy about baseball. I drift away until I find a bench.

If Mom were here, she'd be complaining about the shoes she'd worn. Always a trend setter but not a practical one. Dad would offer to carry her on his back. She'd deny him, of course, because he was always in pain. Hudson would kick off his tennis shoes and offer them to Mom, saying he didn't care if he went barefoot. We'd all laugh—

"Anyone sitting here?" a voice asks.

I look up to see a boy I'd noticed in Amy's store staring at me. He goes to school with me. Travis Mayes. "All yours," I reply.

He sits down and his thigh brushes against mine. "This band sucks."

Laughing, I glance up at the stage. "They do. She likes them, though." I point at Amy as she dances like an idiot. Hudson is still deep in conversation with the one guy.

"You should come with me and my buddies to Club Exodus one night. The bands are way better than this."

"Isn't Club Exodus twenty-one and up?"

His grin is devious. "Before my brother went to prison, he broke into the DMV and stole a bunch of shit. I make fake IDs all the time for my friends." He nudges my shoulder with his. "I could get you one, friend. Whatever you want, I can make it happen. I have my ways, thanks to my brother."

"He sounds like a great influence," I deadpan.

He snorts, but his eyes are twinkling. "My brother taught me everything I know. I'm just smarter than him. If you ever need anything, I can get it for you. I'm cheap too."

"I'll keep that in mind," I say and then groan. "This band really does suck."

"Definitely sucks. By the way, I haven't seen you lately in first hour," he says. "Everything okay besides, you know…?"

I jerk my head over to look at him. "Besides losing my mom and dad on the same night? Everything is peachy."

"I didn't mean it like that," he mutters. "I just wondered how things were at home."

Tears burn my eyes and I choke on my words, irrationally angry at him. "Home? Travis, I have no home. The only home I knew is being rented out by another family now."

"Hey," he tries gently, his hand patting my thigh. "I was only saying—"

"Rylie," Hudson barks.

When I look up, Hudson stands in front of me, his hands fisted at his sides. Fury rolls off him in waves. I can tell he's seconds away from knocking his fist through Travis's nose.

"I'm fine," I croak out.

Travis jerks his hand away and rises to his feet. "I'll see you around, Rylie."

Hudson, with his jaw clenched, watches Travis until he disappears into the crowd. Then, he turns his intense glare my way.

"Aren't they great?" Amy says as she dances over to us. Her big boobs bounce and I hate her. I hate her because she's been with my brother. He's been inside her. I hate her for that.

"Yep," Hudson and I both answer at the same time.

He smirks at me and we share a silent moment. The band sucks.

"Let's dance." She grabs his hands and tries to get him to move to the music.

"Actually," he says with a frown. "Aunt Becky called. She wants Rylie to come home. It's getting late."

"Oh." Her bottom lip pouts out. "I'll see you tomorrow then?"

"Yeah, of course."

She stands on her toes and runs her fingers through his hair, drawing him to her mouth. They kiss and I want to throw up. I hurry to my feet and start for the truck to give them their privacy. But before I get too far away, Hudson falls into step beside me.

"You didn't have to stop making out on my account," I say bitterly.

He doesn't say anything until we're in the parking lot, walking between cars. We find his truck, but he doesn't get in. Instead, he follows me over to my side and stops me before I can climb inside.

"Who was that guy?" he demands.

I stare at him with my mouth hanging open. "Travis? He's a kid from school."

"Stay away from him. He's trouble." He crosses his arms over his chest, accentuating how big his biceps are.

Rolling my eyes, I shove him away from me. "Why do you care?"

He stalks forward and pulls me to him against his solid chest. "Because I do."

I melt against him and wrap my arms around his middle. He hugs me so tight I wonder if he'll crush my ribs. I like it. I like being suffocated by him. His grip relaxes and he rubs my back.

"Come on," he murmurs. "Aunt Becky didn't really call. That music was just shitty and I was so fucking over it."

I laugh as he pulls away and grabs my hand. We link fingers. He guides me between cars until we reach a park. It's dark, but the moon shines down on the playground equipment, giving it a haunted quality.

"Do you remember when you ran away?" I ask him, a giggle tumbling from me.

He flashes me a boyish grin that makes my stomach clench. "I was mad."

"You struck out."

"And, at the time, it was the end of the world."

"Mom was so worried, but I knew where you'd go," I tell him with a smile.

He guides me to the swing set and we both sit down.

"When I saw you, I thought you were there to rat me out," he admits. "But…"

"I was running away too." My voice is cheerful. I remember I packed my little Barbie backpack and filled it with snacks Hudson likes. When Mom was fretting, I snuck away to go find my brother.

"I was mad at first, but then I was happy you were there because I was fucking hungry," he says. "And bored."

I push off on the swing. The wind from the movement makes my dress fly up. A shiver ripples through me. Hudson doesn't move, simply rocks a little in his swing. Pumping harder and harder, I try to see how high I can go. This used to be a game I'd play with myself when I was younger—to see if I could flip all the way around. I never could.

Hudson gets up and walks the perimeter of the playground, his eyes never leaving me. I watch as he climbs the playset like he's a monkey. He disappears inside the tower. When I'm as high as I think I'll go, I jump off the swing and land with a thud. Then, I run after him. I climb to the top and find him sitting with his back against the wood railing. The space is small, but there's enough room for me to sit next to him.

"Rylie?"

"Yeah?"

"My head hurts."

I frown and turn to look at him. "Are you sick?"

His intense green eyes bore into mine. "Very."

"Do you need medicine?"

He shakes his head. "I don't think so."

"I'm sorry."

His hand finds mine and he threads his fingers with mine. "I'm not."

My heart races at his words. "Travis is just some kid from my class. You don't have to…" Be jealous. "Worry."

"I need help," he murmurs. "Advice."

I turn my body and sit cross-legged facing him. "I can try."

His eyes roam from my eyes to my lips to my throat. Then, he rakes them down the rest of my body until they land on our hands. Mine covers his and his has settled on my bare thigh.

"I'm worried about me and Amy," he murmurs. "I think we need a break."

I let out a ragged breath. "How come?"

"I'm too distracted."

"By what?"

"You."

Heat prickles across my skin and I bite on my bottom lip. Embarrassment floods through me, but it's mixed with delight.

"You're smiling," he says and he smiles too. "You're happy."

"I'm not," I lie.

He smirks. "So what do I do about it?"

"I don't know." I shiver. It's not cold, but my nerves are alive.

"Come here," he growls.

I sit up and slide into his lap, straddling him. I wait for him to tell me I'm sitting on him in an inappropriate way, but he rests his hands on my lower back and smiles at me.

Our eyes are locked, but neither of us speaks. He's hard beneath me. My brother's cock is hard because of me. It makes me want to rub against him, but I'm too shy. I don't have the nerve to do it even though I desperately want to.

"Still cold?" he rumbles.

"Kinda," I lie.

I lean forward against his chest and inhale his flesh on his neck. His palms slide to my ass and he pulls me closer. My breath hitches when I rub against his erection through his jeans. He doesn't take his hands off my butt.

"Hudson," I whisper. I want to ask him what's happening. Ask him why I like it so much. If I didn't fear his rejection, I'd ask him if he wants it too.

He pulls me to him again, his fingers digging into my ass. Another mewl escapes me. I rub my lips along his neck. The urge to lick him is overwhelming, but I refrain, just barely.

"Fuck, Rylie." His voice is pained. Fingers bite into me once more as he uses my body for friction. "Fuck."

I lift up to look at him. His green eyes flare with emotion. Need and desire. For me. I'm drunk off the look. I slide my fingers into his hair.

I want to kiss him.

Sick. Sick. Sick.

He grinds me against him again. This time, a loud moan rips from my throat. His wild eyes lock with mine. Pleading and begging. For what? I don't know.

My panties are soaked and I wonder if he can smell my arousal. It's heady and thick in the air. I should be ashamed because he's my brother, but he's got the fever too.

Lost and sick.

Sick and lost.

His palms abandon my ass and then slide up my thighs. Fire blazes in his orbs. I rock against him, urging him on. He groans and his fingers slip under my dress. We both suck in a sharp breath.

"Rylie," he groans.

I dip forward and kiss his lips. Like last night in the tent. Softly. Unsure. And he bites me like he's done before. But this time not on my jaw. On my bottom lip. He lets go and our lips press together again.

I'm on fire.

The fever—this sickness—is maddening me.

I part my lips and breathe into his mouth. I suck in his scent. Steal his air. Devour his groan. His tongue brushes along mine. It's foreign in my mouth, but I like the taste. An instant addiction. I want more.

Two thumbs slide along the seams of my panties on my thighs. I'm in a crazed state because I want him to slip them under the fabric. I grind harder against him, desperate to feel him everywhere.

"Hudson," I murmur against his mouth. "More."

He groans and slides his palms up under my dress to my hips. With his hands, he uses me to dry fuck him. We're both sick, sick, sick. I'm growing dizzy with the need to come. It's more powerful and intense than any time in the shower. This is real. My fantasy come to life.

I'm so close.

So close.

His phone starts ringing and we both freeze. I pull away to find his panicked eyes on mine.

"Fuck," he hisses harshly as he digs his phone out of his pocket. "Yes?" His voice is husky and guilty sounding. One palm is still under my dress on my hip. "W-What? Uh, no.

We took a walk to the park." He pauses. "Aunt Becky will be fine. She trusts me to take care of my sister." Another pause. "Okay, see you in a minute."

He hangs up and his eyes widen. "What the fuck did we just do?"

Guiltily, I slide away from him and right my dress. My panties are soaked and I'm physically throbbing and aching for him. "I don't know."

"I'm sorry," he blurts out as he stands and runs his fingers that were just on my bare skin through his hair. "I'm so fucking sorry."

I'm not.

I stand too and shake my head. "Hudson..."

"Please forgive me," he begs, pain twisting his features.

There's nothing to forgive.

"Hudson!" Amy calls out from somewhere nearby.

His thumb brushes along my chin before he climbs down the playset and runs away from me as though I truly am carrying the sickness.

But he's already caught it.

He's already fucking caught it.

ELEVEN

Hudson

Amy frowns at me as I stride past the swing set toward her.

"Hey," I grunt out, hoping I'm still not sporting an erection.

"Hey." Her gaze flits past me. "Why are you guys out here?"

"Just hanging out," I say, a twinge of annoyance in my voice. "I thought you were staying for the band."

She crosses her arms over her chest and scrutinizes me. "I didn't feel like it without you there. So I was going to my car and saw your truck." Her eyes flit back over to where Rylie is now climbing down from the tower. "Just feels like you were avoiding me."

Rylie walks past us with her gaze down. Guilt is bubbling up inside of me. I'd like to talk to her about what happened just now...what could have happened if we weren't interrupted. Just then, in the heat of the moment, it felt right.

Now it feels all kinds of wrong.

She's my sister.

When she's out of earshot, Amy looks up at me and whispers, "Are we okay?"

I clench my jaw. "I don't think so."

Her big blue eyes quickly fill with tears and spill down

her cheeks. At one time, I hated to see her cry. Now, I find it hard to be moved in any way by her tears. If anything, they're bothering me. "Why? What did I do wrong?"

"It's not you," I assure her. I rub the back of my neck and stare down at our feet. "I did something I'm ashamed of."

"With Rylie?" she breathes, her voice choking up.

I snap my glare to hers, overly protective of Rylie's reputation, and hiss out my words. "No, not my fucking sister," I lie.

"I'm sorry." A sob chokes her. "I never assumed...I just..."

"I cheated on you, Amy."

She blinks at me and her mouth parts. Her bottom lip trembles. "W-What?"

"At school. There was this girl and—"

"No, Hudson," she says as she hugs herself. "No."

"I'm sorry," I mutter. "I fucked up."

"Is this why you've been so distant? Are we breaking up?"

Most girls would flip the hell out and break up with their boyfriend about now. Not Amy. God, why does she have to be so forgiving? She doesn't deserve someone who not only cheated on her but did it again with his own sister.

"Amy..." I don't know what we're doing.

"We can fix this," she assures me through her tears, her shaky hands reaching for my belt. "I can do the things you like. I'm sorry, Hudson. I'll give you blow jobs again like you want. Please." A loud, ugly sob escapes her.

Gently, I push her hands away from me. For so many reasons. Reasons I can't even unpack from my mind right now. "No, Amy. A blow job won't fix everything. It's not that easy."

"I love you, Hudson. Whatever it is you're dealing with, we can get through it together."

Not this.

I don't know how to deal with this.

Confusing thoughts about my sister.

What Rylie and I just did…

That kiss.

The way she rubbed on me.

My cock twitches at the reminder and I groan, running my fingers through my hair.

Amy throws her arms around my neck and hugs me, bawling her eyes out. "I can't lose you. We've been through so much together. Please, Hudson."

I hug her because she deserves the comfort, but I'd rather be hugging someone else. "I'm sorry, Amy. I just need to figure some shit out." Figure out how not to want to fuck my sister.

She sobs but nods. "I'll be here for you."

I stroke her hair and let out a heavy sigh. "Let me walk you back to your car."

"I'm sorry," she whispers again.

I'm sorry too.

I stand under the spray of the shower with my head bowed. The drive home tonight, Rylie and I didn't say a word. I wanted to say a lot of things, but my mind was a mess. The moment we got back, she bolted from the truck and disappeared.

The water eventually runs cold and I'm forced to get

out. I dry off and wrap the towel around my waist. When I step out of the bathroom, Rylie sits perched on the arm of the sofa. Her long, slender legs are bare and I can't help but glance over them.

"Rylie," I start.

She stands up and walks over to me. I can see her small nipples through her white T-shirt. Her black cotton shorts are short and draw attention to her tanned legs. A sharp breath hisses from me when she stands too close. Not close enough that we touch, but close enough that I can smell her clean hair.

"You said you'd shave me," she murmurs, her voice low and intoxicating. It slides over my skin like warm wax. A little painful at first, but then it feels good.

I'm not supposed to feel this way about my fucking sister.

"I did," I agree, my tone gruff. "Let me throw on some pants."

After a beat of silence, she nods. I stalk from the bathroom over to my drawers and yank out a pair of gray sweats. She's gone into the bathroom, so I drop the towel and then slide the sweats on. When I walk back into the bathroom, she's sitting perched on the edge of the sink. I close the door and lock it behind me. The room feels too small with both of us in it.

I can't meet her eyes as I reach past her to plug the sink and turn on the warm water. Her intense stare bores into me. I can feel the heat of it burning me. Quickly, I grab my can of shaving cream and my razor.

"I think I broke up with Amy," I blurt out as I turn off the water once the sink is filled.

"Oh?" Her voice is small. "I'm sorry."

I give her a nod and then tap her knee with my knuckles. "Stretch your leg across the sink," I instruct, my voice husky.

She complies and my cock takes notice of her spread open before me, her shorts the only thing between us. I cup my hand in the warm water and release it on her leg. Her breath hitches when I palm her leg, wetting it. I run my palm over her knee, along her thigh, and stop just below the hem of her shorts. It takes intense focus, but I manage to pull my hand from her leg to squirt some shaving cream into it. I rub the cream along her shin and start spreading it over her flesh.

"You're so hairy," I tease, hoping to break up the intense moment.

She laughs, soft and breathy. "Good thing you're going to take care of me."

I drag my gaze to her pretty brown eyes. "I'll always take care of you."

Her pink cheeks turn redder and she smiles.

With my eyes back on her leg, I rub more cream over her knee and thigh. Once I'm done, I rinse off my hand and grab the razor. Before I start, I give her a crooked grin. "Trust me?"

"Of course," she murmurs.

Slowly, I run the razor up along her shin. Aside from our heavy breathing, all that can be heard is the crackling as the razor cuts through her hairs and leaves smoothness in its wake. I stop at her knee and rinse it off. I'm lost to my task when I accidentally nick her knee. She lets out a hiss.

"Shit," I grumble. "I'm sorry."

I continue shaving the rest of her leg. The blood trickles down the inside of her knee. Not enough to drip into the sink but enough to make me feel bad. With quick movements, I rinse away the leftover shaving cream. Then, I snag a towel from the hanger and wipe away the excess water. The cut continues to bleed. I hold the towel to it and regard her with regret.

"I shouldn't have kissed you," I murmur. "That was wrong."

Her brows furl together and her voice is a whisper. "But I liked it."

My heart seizes in my chest. "Rylie, I liked it too."

"*But?*" she rasps out.

"But it's wrong."

She shuts down and breaks eye contact. Her sadness and loneliness seem to crash into me like a giant wave, knocking me over. The urge to make her happy again is overwhelming. I bend over and kiss her cut. Then, I lick the metallic taste from her flesh.

When I pull away and look at her, a shy smile tugs at her lips.

My shame over what we did doesn't matter when I can wipe away her sadness with one simple act. It's wrong and yet it fixed her so quickly.

"Let's shave the other leg," I grunt out. My cock is semi-erect in my pants and I wonder if she notices.

I'm more careful this time and manage to keep from cutting her. When I'm finished and have wiped her clean, I chance a look at her. Her brown eyes blaze with emotion. The same look she gave me when she was grinding on my cock hours ago. It's maddening to stare at her plump parted lips and not kiss them. Fuck, how I want to kiss them.

She slides off the countertop and stares up at me, a shy smile tilting her lips. I'm fucking mesmerized. "Hudson?"

"Yeah, Ry?"

"You'll shave under my arms too?" A crimson blush paints her throat and I crave to press my lips to her flesh to see if she feels warm there as well.

"Would you like me to?" I ask, my voice low and throaty.

"Yes," she breathes.

My gaze skims over her shirt. "You'll have to take that off."

Her stare is intense as she nods. "Okay, but don't make fun of me."

"Make fun of you?" I ask in confusion, my brows furling together.

"I'm not big like Amy."

Her breasts.

Fuck no, I won't be making fun of them. I can't stop thinking about them.

"I won't make fun of you," I vow.

She bites on her bottom lip and grips the hem of her shirt. My cock aches in my sweats as I watch her slowly peel it up, baring her stomach to me. When the curves of the bottoms of her bare breasts come into view, I let out a groan. Then, I'm rewarded a view of her dark pink, small, erect nipples.

Fuck.

She pulls the shirt off and drops it to the floor. I can't help but advance on her. I need to inhale her and taste her and touch her.

"Raise your arm," I instruct, my gaze still on her perfect tiny tits.

She obeys and I step closer until my erection presses against her. I have the razor in my left hand, but my right hand is curious. I raise it and grip her nipple between my knuckles. Small. Hard. Erect. The craving to bite them is overwhelming.

"Rylie," I murmur as I pull gently on her nipple with my knuckles. "My sweet Rylie."

Her fingers run their way into my hair and she draws me to her. Our breath comingles as we grow infected by the sickness we're both so clearly ailed by. Many dirty thoughts tease and taunt me. I want to do so many bad things to her. So many bad things that will make her feel good.

"We can't do this," I tell her, even as I twist her nipple slightly.

Her breath hitches. "Nobody has to know."

How fucking tempting is that?

"You're my sister." It's a reminder we both need to hear.

"But it feels good, Hudson. *We* feel good."

I tear my gaze from hers to stare down at her breasts. The nipple in my grip is so responsive to my touch. The urge to taste her is strong. I hesitate and pull my hand from her. When I start to pull away, her body seems to deflate. Shame. Not at what we're doing but shame for herself. She feels rejected. My mind wars between right and wrong. I know what feels right…it just happens to be wrong.

Nobody has to know.

I dip down and run my nose along the outside of her breast. Her skin is so soft. My mouth waters.

Nobody has to know.

Flicking my tongue out, I give in. I run it up her silky young skin and seek out her peaked nipple. When the tip of my tongue rubs over her areola, she lets out a harsh breath. I tease the tip of her small nipple and smile when she lets out a sweet, quiet moan. I grab her small breast and squeeze it so I can suck her into my mouth. Her breathing is loud and raspy, but she's into it. She grips my hair and holds me to her as if I might pull away at any moment. As I suck her tit, I rub my tongue back and forth across her flesh. She lets out a garbled sound when I gently bite the hardened peak before sucking her hard again. I pop off her and admire how red and splotchy her skin is now.

"Beautiful," I murmur. I blow a breath on her wet skin and she shivers. "You taste good." Slowly, I press kisses from one breast to the other. I tease and suck on it until it too is red and matches its twin.

When I look up at her, her plump lips are parted and her brown eyes are liquid chocolate as lust swims in her gaze. I'm caught off guard when her lips crash to mine. Awkward at first as her teeth bump against my lips, but then we're both opening to seek out the other. My moan mixes with hers as I inhale her. She tastes like toothpaste and I want to suck on her tongue for hours. The razor falls to the ground with a clatter as I abandon it to grab two fistfuls of her tiny ass. I lift her and she wraps her skinny legs around my waist. She's so light. Worry, once again, niggles at me, wondering if she's eating enough. But the moment her bare breasts press against my naked chest, I'm distracted by her.

Nobody has to know.

I kiss her hard and press her back into the wall. Gripping her ass, I use her body to grind against my cock through my sweatpants.

"I want more," she begs against my lips.

Fuck, I do too.

"You and I can't do this." I pull away far enough so I can see her. "We're—"

She slaps at the wall beside her and then we're shrouded in darkness. "We're not them. We're Hudson and Rylie.

Two people who want to be together like this." Her teeth find my lip in the dark and she tugs. "In the dark, we can be whoever we want to be. In the dark, we can make love. Nobody has to know."

I can't see her, but I can feel and taste and smell her. She slides her legs down until she's standing and then her small hands are blindly searching for the waistband of my sweatpants. A loud groan escapes me when she pushes down. My cock, thick and eager, springs free. When her soft hand grips my erection, I let out a ragged, harsh breath.

"Rylie," I plead.

She strokes me and it makes me desperate for more. She's right. In the dark, we can be whoever the fuck we want to be. I want to devour every part of her. As she strokes me, I slide my palms into the back of her shorts. The skin of her bouncy ass feels like silk. I grip her flesh and spread her cheeks apart, loving the mewls escaping her. Then, I slip them back out before pushing her shorts down her thighs.

"Nobody has to know," I utter, as though I need to remind myself.

"Nobody," she agrees.

Our lips find each other again as my palm slides down her taut stomach toward her pussy. My fingertips have just brushed against her thatch of pubic hair when someone pounds on the bathroom door. I jerk away from Rylie as my heart nearly jumps from my throat.

"Hudson!" Aunt Becky shrieks. "Rylie is gone! I think she's run away." The door handle jiggles and then she says, "Are you sitting in the dark?"

Fuck. Fuck. Fuck.

I yank my sweats up and flick the light on. "No. The light is on." I glance at Rylie and she scrambles to put her shirt back on.

"Rylie's gone," Aunt Becky exclaims.

"She's fine," I mutter. "I was helping her with something."

Rylie shoves the shirt over her head and then her arms through the holes. I rake my eyes over her tits that are still red from my mouth before she pulls the shirt down over them.

Aunt Becky's silence is momentary and then her icy voice hisses through the door. "Open this door right now, Hudson Hale, or so help me I'll get Randy down here and—"

I unlock the door and open it. Aunt Becky glares at me, her arms crossed over her chest. Her eyes take in my appearance. My hair hasn't been combed from my shower earlier. I'm probably still sporting a boner. And I'm half dressed.

Her eyes dart over to Rylie, who nervously tugs at the bottom of her shirt but won't meet Aunt Becky's stare.

"What were you two doing in here?" Aunt Becky demands.

"She wanted to shave her legs and I didn't want to leave her alone with the razor." Mostly the truth.

"This is extremely inappropriate," she bites out. "You're both practically naked."

Anger swells up inside me and I glower at her. "Stop," I snap. "Stop whatever you're insinuating. She's my fucking sister."

"Watch your tone, Hudson. I may be legally responsible for her, but I took you in because I love you, not because I have to. If I think Rylie's safety is in jeopardy, I will send you—"

"My *safety* in jeopardy?" Rylie asks, her voice shrill. "You're being crazy, Aunt Becky! He's my brother!"

"Which is why you two don't need to be locked in a dark bathroom together missing half your clothes," Aunt Becky screams, throwing her hands up in the air in frustration. "Rylie, go to your room. Now."

Rylie's eyes are watery and she shoots me a questioning look. I give her a small nod. She pushes out of the bathroom and leaves us be. The basement door slams behind her.

Gritting my teeth, I pick up the razor and toss it into the sink. Aunt Becky steps aside and I storm over to the dresser to hunt for a shirt.

"I know you two are hurting over your parents and then after what happened with Rylie but…" she trails off.

I whip around and frown. "But what?"

"But *that* can't happen."

"Me helping my sister? Me comforting her? And why the hell not?" I demand, my fury making my entire body tremble.

She shakes her head at me. "I'm not stupid. Whatever was going on in there was far from innocent. It was written all over both your faces." Her nostrils flare. She's disgusted with me.

"I have a girlfriend. I'm not fucking my sister," I snarl as I storm over to my bag. No, I just wanted to. "I'm leaving."

She lets out a heavy sigh. "That's probably for the best. Put some space between you two. You've spent too much time together."

I don't answer her as I pack a bag.

I don't even get to say goodbye to my sister.

TWELVE

Rylie

"Rylie," Aunt Becky says, her voice soft from the doorway. "We need to talk."

I watch through the window Hudson's taillights until they disappear. The moment they're gone, I feel empty. An ache forms in my chest. I want to call him, but I knew this conversation would happen after she busted us.

My heart flutters at the still-fresh memory of holding his hot, rigid cock in my hand. I wanted to explore every part of him. Taste every inch. The sickness that simmers below my surface is bubbling more and more each day. Tonight, it splashed over onto Hudson.

We kissed.

We touched.

Tonight was ours.

"So talk," I bite out.

She lets out a heavy sigh and sits on the bed. Despite her wearing her frilly pajamas, she resembles Mom and it makes my heart clench in my chest. When she's being nice and caring, she's a lot like my mother. In some ways, it makes me happy. In other ways, it makes me sad. It's a reminder my mom is no longer here. Neither is Dad. It's just me and Huds. Until the end.

"I need you to tell me what happened."

I tense and cross my arms over my chest. "He helped me shave my legs."

Our eyes meet and hers narrow as she studies me.

"It was inappropriate," she clips out.

"He's my brother."

We have a silent standoff before she softens again.

"Did he, um, touch you?" Her brows furl together and she swallows.

"He had to touch me," I deadpan. "He was shaving my legs."

She bristles and straightens her back. "You know what I mean. Did he touch you inappropriately?"

Nobody has to know.

"No," I lie, keeping my features impassive. At least I hope she can't see through my mask.

"Good, because you're still a minor and that could land him in jail, Rylie. Not to mention, there are laws about siblings being together in that way."

I glower at her. "In what way?"

"Sexually. Romantically. You were both practically naked sitting in the dark. I think because emotions are running high since the loss of your parents, that you're both—"

"Stop," I snap. "Don't go there. You're being disgusting. I would never do that and neither would Hudson. Do you think we're sick?"

Sick. Sick. We're definitely sick.

"No, but I just think—"

"Well, stop thinking," I choke out. "I won't have you making Hudson feel bad for trying to comfort me."

She rises from the bed and walks over to me. "Okay then. Perhaps I misread the situation. I'm not good at this parenting thing. I only want to protect you as your parents would have."

"Who will protect Hudson?" I croak out.

Me. The answer is me.

"He's a grown man now," she says softly. "He can take care of himself."

"Are we done here?" I ask, tears threatening. "I'm tired."

She nods and slips out of my room without another word. Once I'm certain she's gone back to her room, I grab my phone and hide in my closet in the dark. I turn it on and dial my brother. He answers on the first ring.

"Hey," he says, his voice gravelly, sending a thrill right down my spine.

"Hey. Where are you going?"

He lets out a heavy sigh. "Amy's, I guess."

I wince. "I thought you two broke up."

"Maybe we shouldn't have," he whispers. "Maybe I shouldn't have done a lot of things tonight."

My chest aches like someone is taking a bat to it. Pounding. Over and over again.

"Don't say that." A tear races down my cheek.

"Rylie…" His teeth grind loudly together. "We fucked up."

"Nobody has to know."

He's silent for a beat. "It's illegal."

"I'll be eighteen soon."

"No, it's illegal because we're brother and sister. We could go to prison for up to four years. I looked it up."

I laugh because it's absurd. "We didn't do anything wrong."

"And we won't," he grumbles. "It's better this way. I'm sorry."

"But I liked it…"

He exhales heavily. "I liked it too. But we can't. It's wrong and against the law. We just need some space and things can go back to the way they used to be."

"I don't want things to go back to the way they were," I say sharply. "I don't want to lose you."

"Hey," he murmurs. "I'll still be here. As your brother. We just can't…"

Touch. Kiss. Fuck.

"Okay." It's the answer he wants. The only answer I can give him apparently. But it is not okay. I've had a taste of him and I'm poisoned by the thought of more.

"We'll still talk and share music," he assures me. "But…" He sighs. "I'm going to try and make things right with Amy. It has to be this way." His voice cracks and I want to reach through the phone to hug him. He deserves so much more than Amy. He deserves me.

"She's going to be so happy," I groan, jealousy already eating away at my heart.

He chuckles. "Yeah."

"She's going to cry."

"That's a given."

We both grow quiet.

"Rylie?"

"Yeah, Huds?"

"In another life…I would want it." He lets out a frustrated huff. "I would find a way to make it happen."

Just not *this* life.

A sniffle. "Night, Hudson."

A sigh. "Night, heathen."

I can't breathe.

This sickness is slowly suffocating me.

Second by lonely second.

His voice on the phone isn't enough.

For three days, I've spent my spring break curled up in my bed wearing a hoodie Hudson left as I sleep my woes away. In my bed—in the darkness—I'm free to imagine the other life. The life Hudson promised he'd find a way if there were one. In that life, we kiss and touch. In that life, we make love.

I've become obsessed with the idea of him and me.

Of his naked body pressed against mine, his hard cock rubbing between us. Our lips pressed together. Tongues tasting and tangling. His scent filling my lungs and never leaving.

I can't cry anymore.

I did that for two days. Today, I'm numb. I miss him.

Hudson: How are you holding up today, heathen?

The screen blurs as tears well up in my eyes. Apparently I'm not all cried out. Knowing he hates the thumbs-up, I send him that emoji. I get the middle finger emoji back, which makes me laugh. The first laugh in days.

Me: I miss you.

He doesn't reply and the tears silently leak from my eyes, wetting the pillowcase below. The nice thing about spring break is that my aunt and uncle are busy at work. I'm left alone to wallow in my despair. Nobody forces me to dress or shower or eat. I'm left alone.

Too alone.

I drift in and out of sleep, my dreams confusing me and teasing me.

"Rylie."

His voice is so real. I want to hear him say my name over and over again.

"Rylie." This time it's barked out, borderline angrily.

Turning in bed, I lock eyes with the concerned ones of my brother. Like glowing green orbs in the darkened bedroom.

"What are you doing? It's spring break. You should be out doing things," he mutters, his voice husky.

I shrug. "We were supposed to spend the break together doing things. Without you, I have no one to do them with."

He frowns and sits on the edge of my bed. So close. I could reach out and link my fingers with his. But I don't. He's drawn the line in the sand and he wants me to stay on my side.

In another life…

This life requires lines.

This life says we must obey laws.

He reaches over and grabs my hand. "Rylie."

I'm focused on the strength and heat emanating from his grip. The way he holds me in an intimate way despite the line he drew. My heart flutters inside me.

"Hudson."

"Let's get out of here. I'll take you to a movie or some-thing. You need to get out of bed," he says, his thumb swip-ing over the back of my hand. Chills race up my arm from his touch and I shudder. He seems to think I'm cold because he lets go of my hand long enough to curl up beside me on the bed. A strong, warm, heavy arm drapes over my waist. Now that we're so close, just inches away, I could almost kiss him. The line he drew has already been crossed.

I reach up to touch his face and he winces. It's enough to have me jerking it back and balling my hand into a fist.

"How's Amy?" I ask coolly.

He lets out a sigh. "She's fine."

"Back together and happily ever after on the horizon?"

"Hardly." He chuckles. "She surprised us both, Ry. Cried, yes, but give in? Nope. She says I have some soul searching to do. That maybe I need to get out there and see other people too. Then, once I've had my fill, she'll be waiting. She said she doesn't want me to always feel like I never had a chance to date and experience other women."

I lift my brows in surprise. "So you're…"

"Still seeing each other but also seeing other people."

"Like the girl from school?"

"Jada? I don't know. I mean, she's nice, but…" he drifts off.

But you want me instead?

I glance up to meet his intense stare. "But what?"

"But that won't make me happy." He frowns. "I'm struggling here." His palm cups my cheek and he runs his thumb along my cheek. "I know what I want…"

Me. He wants me.

"I'm tired," I whisper tearfully.

Tired of this fight. Tired of the sadness. Tired of a life where the design wasn't clean and neat, but messy and fragmented. I'm just tired.

"I know you are," he murmurs. He leans forward and kisses my forehead.

I choke back a sob. My fingers tangle in the front of his T-shirt as I clutch him to me, desperate for the connection with my brother. He doesn't resist and hugs me the rest of the way to him. With his arm holding me close, I relax for the first time in days. Ugly sobs rip from my chest and he rubs my back as though that might soothe the pain away.

In another life…

He rolls onto his back but maneuvers me so I'm half draped over his solid frame. His scent is dizzying me. Masculine and clean. I could inhale him all day long and get high.

"It'll be hard sorting through this," he explains as though he has all of life's answers. "We can do it together. We're both stronger than the feelings we're having."

Bitterness creeps up inside me. He may have this life's answers, but I have the other life's answers. In the other life, we're best friends and lovers. We can kiss and fuck. We can marry and have children. We can love in *that* life like no siblings can love in *this* life. That life holds the happily ever after I'll never get to see.

"I can't lose you," I mutter. "I'll take you however I can get you."

He runs his fingers through my tangled hair. "Me too, baby, me too."

I cry, but he remains strong. Unbreakable. Solid. My brother, the hero.

"Let it all out," he urges. "And then I'm going to fill you back up with popcorn, peanut M&Ms, and whatever action movie that's playing at the theater."

"And an Icee. I want a cherry Icee," I tell him through my tears.

"I'll give you whatever you want."

Except us.

He can't give me us.

THIRTEEN

Hudson

Three weeks later…

"Coach was pissed," Nick says when he comes sauntering out of the bathroom of the hotel room we're sharing, a towel wrapped around his waist.

I groan and scrub my palm over my face. "I fucked up. Whatever. I'll do better next weekend."

He drops his towel, showing me his hairy ass as he hunts for something to wear in his suitcase. Once he throws on some jeans, he levels me with a serious stare. Nick is hardly ever serious. "I think he'll bench you."

Irritation bubbles up inside me. "Well, he can fucking bench me then."

"Or," he says as he pulls on a T-shirt, "you could get your head out of your ass."

Leaving me with those words, he walks back into the bathroom to spend far too much time for a man on his hair. I've showered but only dressed in sweats after the game. I'm not going out no matter how much Nick pressures me.

The game was a fucking nightmare. I couldn't catch anything that was slung my way and I couldn't hit worth a shit. All I could think about was her.

My sister.

Rylie had texted before the game telling me about how

some kids from school invited her to a party. She didn't want to go, but Aunt Becky of all fucking people urged her to get out of the house and socialize.

I lean back against the pillows and read her newest text.

Rylie: Travis is here.

Jealousy flares as I think about the kid from the downtown block party. I didn't like the way he looked at her. Like he wanted her. She's not his.

She's mine.

But she's not. She can't be. Having Aunt Becky nearly busting us was enough to scare the shit out of me. I'd lost my head and nearly fucked my sister. My dick twitches at the reminder. Her hand was so soft wrapped around my cock. I still think about her tiny nipple trapped between my teeth when I jack off in the shower. Truth is, I can't get that night out of my head. I'm trying to be reasonable here and do the right thing. Because we wouldn't just be social pariahs, we'd be breaking the law.

Fucking Missouri.

I dig my laptop out of my bag and pull up the website where I'd learned we could get up to four years in prison for incest. That's what it is after all. Incest. It's fucking unfair that aggravated rape only pulls in one more year in prison for a punishment but loving your sister is nearly an equal crime. What Rylie and I want to do is consensual. Safe. Doesn't harm fucking anyone. According to the website, she's of legal age of consent anyway. She's just born with the wrong last name. The *same* last name. The same damn genetic makeup.

Clicking on Arkansas, because everyone always makes fun of people fucking their cousins there, I'm irritated to learn the law isn't much different than ours. I expand my search to Kansas and Mississippi, finding more of the same. Oklahoma seems to have one of the more lenient punishments, but when I click on Montana, I lose my shit.

"No less than life imprisonment or one hundred goddamned years? Are you kidding me?" I roar as I nearly throw my laptop into the floor in fury.

Nick rushes from the bathroom and nosily looks at my screen before I can close it. "Incest laws? What the fuck, man?"

"Research paper for Ritter's class," I lie, anger still exploding inside of me. "You can't marry your cousin or else spend your life in prison but, according to Montana, you only get up to ten years for making child porn. What kind of fucked up world do we live in?"

He laughs. Fucking laughs. "I don't know, Hale. Fucking your cousin is some sick shit. Those nasty rednecks need to rot in jail. We don't need them diluting the gene pool and sending halfwits into the world. There are enough brainless idiots running around this country."

I glower at him. "It's all societal bullshit."

"Still fucking disgusting. Ritter's an asshole for making you guys research this shit. If you need an example, send him a picture of Scottie Brown. That guy looks inbred." He snorts. "I bet his mom fucked her brother. Nobody is that stupid without some tampering with the gene pool."

Despite what Nick says, our team's second baseman is not stupid. He's better looking and a better ball player, which means it gets Nick's jealous panties in a wad.

"There's no proof that fucking your brother makes you have dumb kids," I grit out.

He shrugs as he walks back into the bathroom again to fuck with his hair some more. "That's surprising. But it'd sure make you ugly."

"How do you figure?"

He leans out of the bathroom to shoot me a look of disgust. "Any kid who's born to that shit is gonna get beat up every day of his pathetic life. One too many broken noses because your mommy likes to do her brother will make a kid ugly." He finishes in the bathroom and stuffs his wallet in his back pocket. "You not coming out tonight? I met a couple of hot chicks in the lobby. Gina and Jillian. I'll be a good best friend and let you choose your own adventure." His brows waggle up and down.

"If I don't pass this class, Coach will really kick me off the team. I'll have to catch you next time," I mutter as I snap my laptop closed.

He swipes his keycard off the dresser and shakes his head. "Your loss, man. But when I bring them both back to the room, you stay in your bed. I won't share then."

"Got it," I grumble.

As soon as he's gone, I text Rylie.

Me: I don't like him. Be safe.

The dots move on the screen as I stretch back out on the bed.

Rylie: He's nice. I gave him a hundred bucks to get me a fake ID.

Me: What the hell do you need a fake ID for?

Rylie: So I can go to bars with you once I move out of this dumb hell hole.

I relax at her response. The idea of her going out with Travis pisses me off. But the idea of Ry and me bar hopping together isn't a bad one.

Me: As long as you promise to only go with me, heathen.

Rylie: I wouldn't dream of going with anyone else.

And this is where shit gets hard. Literally. I'm imagining a night of drinking and dancing at the night clubs. Rubbing against her as we dance. Dragging her to a dark corner, lifting her dress, and fucking my sweet sister against a dirty bar wall.

I slide my hand into my sweats and grip my aching cock. With my free hand, I text her back.

Me: I fucking miss you. Three weeks is too long.

Rylie: If Aunt Becky would kindly remove her claws from me, I'd drive down there when you get back from traveling and see you.

Imagining Rylie in my dorm room gets me hot, but then I'm instantly pissed thinking of Nick hitting on her. I know him. He'd try to fuck her and then I'd have to fuck him up.

Me: Call me when you get home. I've had a bad day.

My phone rings and I chuckle. "Yeah?"

"What's wrong?" Her voice is breathy and concerned. It makes my cock twitch in my grip.

"I played like shit. Coach is mad as hell."

"Oh, Hudson," she murmurs. Someone says something to her and she explains she has to take an important call. The music becomes muted and I hear a door shut. "That's better. This party is lame anyway. I'd rather talk to you. Tell me what happened."

I tell her every shitty play and she listens quietly.

"And then I was researching some stuff…" I trail off. "It just put me in a bad mood."

"So you wanted to hear my voice to cheer you up?" she teases.

"You're the only voice who cheers me up."

"How are you and Amy?"

My cock softens in my hand and I groan. "We talk here and there. She went out on a date with a guy named Blake."

Rylie snorts. "Ew. She told you about her date?"

"I think she was trying to make me jealous," I admit.

"Were you?"

"I should be. I should be trying to repair what I broke."

"But…" she probes.

Normally, I change the subject and guide us to simpler topics. Ever since the night I had to tell her we couldn't be together like we both obviously wanted, I've been going crazy. Exactly what I'm not supposed to think about is *all* I think about. It had me so distracted during my game that I fucked that up and pissed off my coach.

"Do you think about that night a lot?"

She lets out a ragged breath. "All the time."

"Me too."

Silence fills the air for a long pause.

"I wanted it, Huds. I wanted to have sex with you."

"I did too," I whisper.

"I still want it."

"We can't," I tell her, hoping I sound firm, but my voice quakes.

"I wish we could. I could probably get Travis to take my virginity, but I don't love him. He'd probably—"

I explode with fury. "You're not fucking Travis," I snap. "Never, Rylie. Got it?"

"Okay," she agrees softly. "That night you and I had felt so good. How can something that feels good be considered bad? Why do people care who we love? We're not hurting anyone."

"It's not that simple," I groan, letting my eyes fall shut. I stroke my cock, trying to mimic the way she did it.

"Everything is so fucking complicated."

"I'm touching myself, Huds," she murmurs. "Just talking to you…I get so…" A soft moan escapes her and it makes my cock jerk in my fist.

"Fuck, baby," I hiss. "Don't do this to me."

"Nobody has to know."

Nobody has to know.

"Are your panties wet?" My words are barely audible.

"Yes."

"Just a little bit or soaked all the way through?"

She moans again. "Now that I'm teasing myself through my panties, I can feel the wetness through the fabric. I wish it were you touching me."

"Jesus, I wish that too."

"Are you touching yourself as well?"

"I'm fucking my fist wishing it were yours," I grind out, my voice low and gravelly.

"I wish I could taste you. I wish I could have you. Just once, Hudson. Maybe I wouldn't feel so sick. Maybe you could heal me."

I pump my cock and tense as my orgasm builds. "If we ever crossed the line, there'd be no coming back, baby. We wouldn't heal. The sickness would fucking spread. I can barely think of anything beside you right now. If I actually had you, I'd become obsessed."

A frustrated sound rips from her. "This is torture, dammit! It's not fucking fair!"

"Shhh," I say in a soothing tone. "Someone will overhear you. It's just us right now."

"We're not doing anything wrong."

But we are. It's so wrong. What we want to do is even worse.

"Take your panties off," I demand, desperate to have this moment with her. Tomorrow we can go back to staying away, but tonight, I want this. "If I can't touch you, I want you to do it for me. I want you to tell me every goddamn sensation, Rylie, because I'm going insane not knowing. I want you to push your fingers into your tight, slippery cunt and I want you to taste how sweet you are. I need to know just how good that forbidden fruit tastes. Please."

She gasps and then a slight moan slips from her. My cock is aching in my grip. I close my eyes and think about her perfect pouty lips. I imagine what it would feel like to rub the tip of my dick against her bottom lip. Would she flick her tongue out and lick me? Would she suck me into her throat?

"Fuck," I curse. "Fuck."

"I'm so wet," she whispers. "When I touch myself normally, it doesn't get like this."

"Because it turns you on that I'm over here fisting my cock wishing you were here to do it instead?" My words are clipped and gravelly.

"Y-Yes, I'm very turned on."

"How many fingers are inside your pussy, Ry?"

"One."

"I'll never get to push my thick cock into you, baby, but I want to know what it would feel like. Put another finger in and tell me how it feels," I demand, my balls heavy with the need to come.

"Tight," she breathes. "I have to use the…um…the juices to get it slippery so it'll slide in better."

Fuck me.

"Is it in now?"

"Yes."

"Do the same for that third finger. My cock is much bigger than your little fingers, heathen. But you can pretend it's me, right?"

"I don't want to pretend." The pout in her voice makes me chuckle.

"I don't want to either. Now tell me how it feels."

She breathes heavily. "Like it's too much but not enough. I want…I need…" Her breathing catches and I can tell she's close.

"If I were there, I'd lick your sweet cunt until you screamed. Those juices that are dripping down your fingers wouldn't be a problem. I'd lick you all clean."

"Hudson," she moans. "I want you."

"I want you too, but it can't happen. Stay with me. Play this game with me, please."

"Okay."

"Put me on speaker so I can hear you."

She shuffles and then tells me she's done it.

"Now," I instruct. "Use your other hand to touch your clit. I want you to rub it and pretend it's my tongue, okay?"

"That feels good," she breathes.

"I would do it so much better, baby. So much better. But this is all we have. I want you to keep rubbing and then tell me when you come. I'm barely holding on here by a thread, but the moment you let go, I'm going to come all over my stomach. If you were here, I'd want you to lick my cock clean and—"

"I'm coming!" she cries out.

The sounds from her are so fucking erotic that it tips me over the edge. I close my eyes, imagining her three fingers inside her little pussy as she makes a big mess with her release. It's enough to have me groaning as cum jets from my dick and shoots up my chest, soaking my bare chest. I keep my eyes closed for a moment as I imagine her sweet red tongue running along my happy trail that's splattered with semen. My cock jolts from that image.

When she bursts into tears, I blink open my eyes and shake away my daze.

"What's wrong?" I demand, panic welling inside me. "Did I…Do you regret…"

"W-What? No," she sobs. "I…I just want you back home. May fifteenth is too far away."

My last final is on the fifteenth, so we have about three weeks until the end of the semester. It may as well be three years because it sure as fuck feels that way.

"It's not that far away," I lie.

"I'm lonely without you." She sniffles.

"I'm lonely without you too."

She's silent for a beat. "I miss Mom and Dad. I'm just a responsibility to Aunt Becky and Uncle Randy."

"I miss them too. I could tell Coach that—"

"No," she interrupts, her tone fierce. "You're already in trouble. Missing another game isn't going to help me because that hurts you. I can wait three weeks."

"But your birthday is next weekend."

"You'll still call me, right?" she asks. "Can we…Can we do this again?"

"As long as we don't actually do it, we're not harming anyone or breaking any fucking laws. So if that'll make you happy on your birthday, you bet we're going to do this again." I reach over and grab my towel off the floor to clean off my sticky stomach. "Maybe, if you're a good girl, we can even video chat."

She sucks in a sharp breath. "Really?"

Nothing sounds more appealing than seeing her face when she comes.

"I want to see you. All of you," I admit.

"Nobody has to know," she murmurs.

My phone buzzes with a text.

"Nobody has to know," I agree.

When I pull away to see who texted me, I realize Rylie has sent me a picture. It's a selfie. Her light brown eyes are hooded and sultry. Plump pink lips are parted. But what has me wanting to reach through the phone and grabbing her is the fact her mouth is wrapped around three very wet fingers.

I stare at the picture and burn it into my memory.

"I have to delete this picture," I mutter, really fucking hating that idea.

"I know. But I wanted you to see."

"Beautiful." My word is barely whispered, but she hears.

"Thank you. I love you, Huds."

"I love you too, heathen."

We hang up, but I stare at the picture for hours. I get hard again and I come once more, this time all alone. And then I continue to stare at what I'll never be allowed to have. When I hear giggling many hours later outside my door, I reluctantly delete the picture.

But I'll never fucking delete this memory.

Never.

FOURTEEN

Rylie

"**S**he took my phone!" Hudson yells as he beats on the other side of my door.

My parents, used to our fights, ignore him. I let out a quiet laugh as I sit down on my bed and easily guess his passcode. I'm just tapping on an app I've never seen before when my door handle jiggles.

Oh crap!

Did he steal the key my parents keep to all the doors?

I let out a squeal when the door opens and he steps inside my room, his chest heaving. Hudson is almost eighteen now. He doesn't know I'm sick. I take a moment to appreciate the hard curves of his chest muscles as he closes the door behind him.

Why is he closing the door?

My heart stammers in my chest.

When Mom and Dad aren't home, he lets Amy come over and they lock his bedroom door. I can hear them having sex each time. It's dirty and embarrassing, but I can't not go to his door each time they do it. The sound of their skin slapping together is the most delicious sound I've ever heard.

Are we going to…

His green eyes are flaming with rage and his hair still drips from his recent shower. When his fingers turn the lock, I forget how to breathe.

He's beautiful.

Sick, Rylie, you're sick.

"Get out of my room," I croak, but I don't mean it. Girls who aren't sick say that sort of thing.

"You had no problems going in mine." His jaw clenches with fury. When did Hudson turn into a man? He's every bit as big as Dad, but he's definitely stronger and more defined.

My finger smashes something on his phone because moans start playing from the app. He pounces on me and knocks his phone into the floor.

"Stay out of my room," he snaps, his strong hands easily pinning me to the bed.

I should be arguing with him or yelling at him. Not loving the way his body feels pressed against mine. The app continues to moan, just like Amy does.

"What's that app for?"

"Nothing a little kid needs to worry about."

I huff and struggle to push him off, the anger finally flooding through me. "I'm not a little kid."

Skin starts slapping and the male starts telling the female to take it. Fucking take it. I strain my head to look. I want to see what they're doing. My lips part the moment I see the man pushing his penis inside the woman. He pulls it all the way out and then drives into her. Over and over again. Something hardens against my thigh and I'm no longer interested in the video.

Hudson, who must have been looking at the video too, snaps his eyes back to mine. His cheeks turn pink. It's not the first time I've seen my brother have a boner through his shorts, but it's the first time I ever felt it.

Big.

Hard.

Throbbing.

I want to ask him if he'll pull his basketball shorts down and *let me touch it. Before I can ask those words, he jerks away from me and snatches his phone from the floor. The moans are silenced, but he can't hide the fact he's still hard.*

"Stay out of my room." His words lack their usual venom and then he's gone, closing my door behind him.

Lying back, I close my eyes and let the sickness take over as I pretend it's me in his room the next time and not Amy.

‿♡‿

"Are you listening?" Aunt Becky clips out on the other line, jerking me from the past.

"Uh, yeah, just thinking about Mom and Dad." Not a complete lie.

"Oh, honey," she says softly. Then, she barks out an address to a cab driver. "I'm sorry. If we didn't already spend all this money on this couples retreat, you know Randy and I would be there with you."

Randy agrees loudly so I'll hear.

"And," she continues, "I know Hudson would too if he didn't have a game against Alabama. Once your brother is out of school, we'll have a big barbeque for you like your parents used to. Are you still going to go out with your friends tonight?"

The mention of my parents has my chest aching.

"Yep," I lie again. "They're all waiting for me at the restaurant, but my friend Mandy is picking me up. Oh, she's here."

"Good," she says. "We love you and will see you Monday when you get home from school. Make sure you take the medicine as prescribed. I only left you enough for the days I'm gone. I'm trusting you and I'll check in."

"Okay. Bye."

I hang up and toss my phone away. It hits the carpet with a thud. I'm not going out. I'm not even dressed. After school, I kicked out of my jeans and crawled into bed. Slept. Cried. Got lost in the darkness that's my mind. There will be no birthday parties or anything special. My highlight of this weekend will be when Hudson calls me after his game. He promised we could video chat and—

"Is there a reason you lied?"

I jerk my head to my doorway to find Hudson leaned against the frame, smirking at me. His baseball cap is flipped backward and he's wearing basketball shorts and a black Gap T-shirt Aunt Becky had bought him not long after our parents had died.

My heart rate skyrockets.

He's hot.

And here.

I scramble out of the bed and rush over to him. He laughs when I throw my arms around his neck and squeal. The moment our bodies are pressed together, I need to be closer. And apparently he does too. His large hands cover my ass cheeks over my panties and he lifts me. I wrap my legs around his waist and pull away slightly to look at him. God, he smells good. Masculine and soapy and simply Hudson.

"You're here." I smile at him.

"It's your eighteenth birthday. You think I'd miss that?" His grin is crooked and handsome. I want to spend the next three days just kissing his mouth.

"Won't Coach be mad?" My brows furrow together in realization that he might be in trouble for coming to see me.

He rolls his eyes. "I was benched anyway."

"Are you upset?"

His green eyes twinkle. "Not anymore."

My heart soars. I can't help myself. Leaning forward, I peck his lips. He doesn't retreat, so I kiss him again, leaving my lips there longer. When I start to pull away, he turns and presses my back against the wall beside my door. His lips fuse to mine and his tongue slides into my mouth as if it belongs there. I welcome it with a moan. Between my spread legs, he grinds his now-hard cock against my aching center. Zings of pleasure flitter through me. I've been dreaming of a million variations of what we're doing since last weekend.

"Where are your pants?" he murmurs against my lips.

"Who cares?"

"Goddammit, Rylie. You're too tempting for me. I'm not strong like I should be." He kisses me hard until we're both panting for air.

"I want you too. It's okay."

He nips at my bottom lip before resting his forehead against mine. His green eyes are intense as he stares me down. "We can't have sex. It's…"

Wrong. He thinks it's wrong. My heart sinks.

"It's illegal," he finishes, but his hips rock against me.

I love the way his hard cock rubs against my clit through my panties. His shorts are thin and I can feel every part of him. It's hot and dizzying.

"Nobody has to know."

He groans as if he's torn. "If we ever crossed that line, I'd never be able to get back over it. I'd want you all the time and then someone would find out, baby. They'd turn us in and take us to jail. I can deal with prison, but you're too sweet and pretty to be locked away." His cock rubs harder and quicker against me. "I can't even think about it."

"This is okay, though, right? We can come without

going to prison," I murmur.

He bites my lip and pulls on it with his teeth before letting go. Fire blazes in his gaze. "Can you come like this?"

"Can you?" I challenge.

He hisses as he works his hips. "I can. I fucking will. I want you to come too."

"Keep doing that and I will."

His mouth presses kisses along my cheek and jaw until he's breathing on my neck near my ear. It's hot and turns me on. I dig my heels into his ass and knock his hat off his head so I can run my fingers through his messy hair.

Like he already knows my body better than I do, he works his hips in a way that has me seeing stars quickly. When I start to shudder, an orgasm nearing, he nips at my earlobe.

"If our lives were different and there weren't stupid fucking laws, I'd pull your wet panties to the side and fuck you raw, Rylie. I'd be the one to take your virginity and earn all your screams of pleasure. You know I would, baby."

His words are too much. I throw my head back and give in to the orgasm that slices through me. He sucks hard on my neck and growls against my flesh. Each thrust becomes erratic and then his cock throbs between us as he reaches his own climax, soaking through his shorts. I turn to mush in his arms and relax. Lazily, he kisses my neck reverently.

"I love you," I whisper.

He pulls away, his green eyes glimmering with an emotion I know is mirrored in my own gaze. "I love you too."

My legs slide down and I stand. His eyes never leave mine as he slides his hand under my T-shirt and touches my pussy over my panties.

"Soaked, heathen. You're a mess." His devilish smirk has

my knees buckling. He pulls me against him as his grin widens. "You're going to have to get cleaned up. I'm taking you out, birthday girl."

I blink at him. "You are?"

"I promised you a tattoo. Unless you've chickened out?" He laughs and starts clucking like a chicken.

"No, I didn't chicken out, asshole." I give him a playful shove. "I'm getting our last name in a pretty script along my ribs." I run my finger along the spot.

His gaze darkens as he rakes his gaze over my nipples that are hard and poking through my shirt. "What should I get?"

"You're really going to get one?"

"Yep. Does it make me stupid if I want the same one?"

Tears prickle at my eyes. "We're the only Hales left. It's not stupid, Huds."

He reaches up and runs a knuckle along my cheekbone, swiping away the rogue tear. "Well, good. Because I was going to get it anyway." He motions at his shorts. "I need to shower. Give me a half hour and I'll be ready to go."

I grab a fistful of his T-shirt and pull him to me. "I could shower with you."

His nostrils flare and his eyes flicker with desire. It makes me shiver. "I think that's a very bad idea."

Frowning, I look away, embarrassed. "Oh."

He grips my jaw and tilts my head up. His lips press to mine gently. "Not because I don't want to. I really fucking want to. It's a bad idea because I'd do that very thing that will get us sent to prison. I'd fuck you, Rylie. I'd fuck you and there would be no turning back."

I swallow and try to look away, but his gaze is locked with mine. "No one would ever know," I remind him. "I'd deny it until the day I died. Don't you trust me?"

"Of course I trust you. I don't trust me."

"You'd tell on us?"

He releases my jaw and kisses me again. So sweet. "No, I'd just not be able to stop touching you and kissing you and loving you for all to see. There would be no hiding it and that would be very bad for us."

I infected him, but now he's sicker than me.

FIFTEEN

Hudson

The entire drive from Arkansas to Missouri, I promised myself I'd keep my distance. I'd see her but not touch her. All that flew out the damn window the moment I caught her looking so fucking sad on the bed. Alone. On her birthday. Before she flew into my arms, half naked, I knew my pep talk was pointless.

I want Rylie so much it's making me fucking crazy.

It's more than wanting what I'm not supposed to have.

It's just her.

Her scent. Her rare smiles. Her wide pale brown eyes. Her luscious lips. Her sweet voice. Her fucking everything.

For years I was with Amy and most of those I swore I was in love with her. But the buzzing in my veins when I'm with Rylie is unlike anything I've ever felt before. She's all I can think about. All I care about. What I have for her is more than love. Not only do we have the love and attraction and chemistry between a man and a woman, but we also have the same history and familial experiences added on top. Maybe that's why incest is frowned upon. A double dose of love. A lethal amount of love. But too much love seems like a good problem to have.

Dinner was nice. I took her to the same Italian restaurant my parents had been headed to when they were killed in the accident. Because of Rylie's new fake ID, we were both able to drink wine in their honor. We reminisced and celebrated like our parents would have wanted us to.

"You're quiet. Are you nervous?" Rylie asks from the passenger seat of my truck.

I squeeze her hand that's tight in my grasp, resting on my lap. "I'm not nervous. Are you sure you want to do this?"

She nods. "I'm ready."

I flash her a grin as I pull into a spot in front of the tattoo parlor. As soon as I shut off the car, I bring her hand up and kiss her knuckles before releasing her. "You look nice. Too nice," I grumble.

Her laugh is musical and so fucking sweet. "Thanks, I think."

My eyes rake over her navy-blue dress that hugs her thin body. It's strapless and the small swell of her breasts gets my cock hard. It'll be difficult to not want to punch fuckers in the face who check her out.

"Before we go in, I wanted to give you your present."

She furls her brows together. "I thought the tattoo was my present."

"That's your other present," I say with a laugh.

I pull the small box from my pocket and hand it to her. "I wanted you to have something that would make you think of me when I wasn't there. And…" I grit my teeth. "And to remind you that if we had a different life, I'd give you everything."

Her throat bobs and her bottom lip trembles as she takes the box from me. She opens it and lets out a gasp. "It's beautiful."

I exhale sharply in relief. "I'm glad you like it. I wanted something simple and not obvious to anyone but us."

She pulls the white gold necklace from the box and

holds it up in front of her. Two gold rings hang from the chain. One is thicker and larger. The other one is thin and dainty. They're wedding bands. Inexpensive. No detail. Simple. But the meaning behind them is everything.

In another life, it could be us.

I don't have to explain it to her, she knows.

Life is unfair. It stole our parents and pushed us together in a way no two siblings are supposed to love. And we can't have it. We're all we have left and we're still as alone as can be.

"Thank you, Hudson," she murmurs tearfully. "Can you put it on me?"

"Of course. Pull your hair up."

She hands me the necklace and then sweeps her hair do the side, exposing her neck to me. It's dark out and we're in a seedy part of town. No one will know. Leaning forward, I kiss her skin where her neck meets her shoulder before I fasten the necklace around her. Once it's in place, the rings hanging down just above her breasts, I run my fingers across her chest before sliding the tip of my pinky through both of the rings.

"It looks good on you." I reluctantly release the jewelry. Once we head inside, I'll have to share her for hours. All I want is to hold her and kiss her, but it's her birthday. She deserves the best birthday. "Let's do this, heathen."

"All done, man. What do you think?" the tattoo artist named Mike asks.

I stand from the chair and walk over to the mirror. When Rylie said she wanted Hale tattooed on her in my handwriting, I decided I wanted to do the same but with her handwriting. The black ink has her neat flourishes scrawled across my ribs. Soon, she'll have a matching tattoo.

"Looks awesome. I love it."

Rylie walks over to me and admires it with a smile. "I love it too."

I give her a wink and her cheeks turn slightly pink.

"Did it hurt?"

"Fuck yes, it did," I say with a laugh. "But you're tough. You've got this."

"You're next, little lady," Mike says and slaps the chair. "I'm going to step out and have a smoke. That'll give you a chance to pull your dress down so I can get to those ribs and get settled." He pulls the door closed behind him.

A flare of jealousy rises up inside of me knowing he'll be touching her bare skin soon.

"You can't murder the tattoo guy," Rylie says, giggling.

Fuck, her giggles are an instant mood lifter. I go from wanting to kill a man to wanting to tickle her just to hear it again.

"Come here," I order, my voice husky.

Her eyes burn with intensity. I know whatever I'm thinking about her, she seems to be mirroring those thoughts. I motion for her to turn her back to me. Gripping the zipper, I tug it down to her ass. The dress starts to slide off, but she holds it to her chest. Her back is naked.

"This dress has a built in bra," she explains.

I splay my palm over her back and run my middle finger down her spine. "I don't like that he'll see you naked."

She turns her head and whispers, "I'm yours, Hudson. Only yours."

My cock reacts, but then I hear Mike talking to someone

just outside the door. I pull my hand away and she settles on the chair. She looks so fucking sexy straddling the chair with her back exposed. I'd give up everything in this world just to be able to claim her as mine. To freely kiss and touch her. To fuck and love her how I want to.

"How big do you want it?" I ask as I pick up the same marker she used for my tattoo and pull off the cap.

"The same size as yours."

I sit on the chair and splay my palm on her back again, thankful for the excuse to touch her. Slowly and carefully, I sign my last name along her ribs. A sense of possessiveness washes over me at seeing my last name on her body.

"I like it," I mutter as I admire my handiwork.

"Then I'll love it."

"Come on," I say as I lock the front door behind us. She giggles as I drag her through the darkened house and into the kitchen. I release her hand to lift the lid off the cardboard container. "What the fuck?"

She turns on the kitchen light. "You got me a cake!" Then her sweet laughter fills the kitchen. "Well, you got Heather a cake."

"That little asshole at the counter had to be told three times how to spell heathen and he still fucked it up." I grumble as I try to drag the pink icing with my pinky on the "r" down to make it look like an "n." "I knew I should have checked it before I left the store."

"It's the thought that counts," she says, her brown eyes twinkling with delight. "Dad was always in charge of the cakes and they always came out special."

I grin because Dad would always get so pissed when they'd fuck the cakes up. But after enough times of us all laughing at his over-the-top reactions, I almost wonder if he didn't sabotage the cakes on purpose after that.

Her smile falls and as she no doubt remembers our father. "I miss him."

"I miss him too." Playfully, I swipe her cheek with the icing on my pinky. Her squeal gets my dick hard.

"You ass!" She swats at me, but I grab her wrist and pull her to me.

"You want me to clean it off?" I tease as I pin her with my hips against the bar. I grip her chin and lick her cheek. She squirms and yells, but the laughter that freely flows from both of us unlocks something inside of me.

Hope. Love. Excitement. Happiness.

All the feelings I danced around my entire life but never partnered up with have finally begun to find their rhythm.

"Don't you want to have more than this?"

"I just love her," I say, trying again, but my argument has weakened.

"But you may not in four years. I want you to experience life a little bit. Then, if Amy and you are still together, I wish you both the best."

Looking back, the way I felt for Amy was strong, but it wasn't this overpowering, thrilling, soul-branding sensation that has burned through me the moment I began to give in to my desires for Rylie.

Rylie is everything.

Her gaze has softened and she's no longer squirming. She's staring up at me as if I'm her whole world. The feeling is mutual. I slide my palms to her face and then thread my fingers into her hair. Tilting her head back, I stare at her plump lips that have now parted. Everyfuckingthing about her is worth my time. I could stare at her all day long and never get bored.

"You're so beautiful," I murmur.

"So are you, Hudson."

Now that we're free of prying eyes, I kiss her slowly. Softly at first. Then, I hungrily nip and suck at her fat bottom lip. Her moans are all for me and I wring more of them from her by the way I easily dominate her mouth. A groan rumbles through me when her palms slide up my chest over my shirt.

I want to do everything with her.

All the things Mom promised were waiting for me.

Why does the universe have to be such a cunt?

This is worse than some cosmic trick. This is cosmic sadism.

Pressing a kiss to the corner of her lips, I murmur out my complaint. "We were meant to be together. I can fucking feel it with everything I am. It's not fair, Ry."

"Nobody has to know," she whispers, her fingers twisting in the fabric of my shirt. "We can kiss and touch and do stuff. We can be together."

"But we can't do *that*," I bite out, the anger for the situation, not her.

"So we won't do *that*, but we can do *this*." She pulls my wrist and I release her hair. I'm guided down to her perky tit over her dress.

"*This* feels fucking perfect," I growl against her lips. Tugging at the top of her dress, I expose her breasts to me. "*This* feels even better." I cup her sweet tit and then rub my thumb over her hardened nipple. "*This* kept me going all those weeks without you. The image of *this* little nipple between my teeth." I pull slightly away and take in the beautiful sight. Her cheeks are flushed and her nostrils flare as she greedily drinks me in. I love that her brown, glossy hair is messy from where I'd been gripping her. I like her messy for me. "I may not be able to fuck you, baby, but I can suck on these until you can't take it anymore."

"It'll never be enough," she cries out when I pinch her.

No, it won't be.

"It's all we have, heathen."

"Then let's take it while we can."

I bend over and bring my mouth to her tit. The nipple is peaked, desperate for attention. Flicking my tongue out, I run it across the bud and taste her. "Fuck, I've missed this."

She whimpers and tugs at my hair. "More."

I chuckle and pull away, regarding her wickedly. "We have all night. But first…" I nod my head toward the cake box. "We have some cake, *Heather*."

An unladylike snort escapes her. "Ugh, fine. Cake first. Teeth later." She pulls her dress back up over her breasts, but my cock doesn't get the memo that we've changed plans.

"You'll be the death of me," I groan.

"You won't get away from me that easy, big brother."

SIXTEEN

Rylie

T he cake is delicious despite it having someone else's name on it. Him going through the effort to get me the cake is much sweeter than the dessert itself. Hudson is back, our aunt and uncle are gone, and we're free to just be. It's the best birthday I've ever had, even if we did have to use plastic utensils because Aunt Becky locked up all the knives before she left.

Once we've eaten our fill on cake and turned all the lights back off, we head upstairs. Hudson grabs his backpack along the way. My nerves are frayed. I just want him so bad that I can barely focus. When we reach my room, he sets his bag on the bed and unzips it.

"Change into something cozy. We're going to watch movies," he tells me as he digs around in the bag.

I huff in frustration. "Maybe I don't want to watch movies."

"Careful, birthday girl," he growls, his green eyes blazing as he looks over his shoulder at me. "I don't want to have to spank you."

"Ha-ha," I deadpan.

He laughs. "There's no rush, heathen. I'm still here. I'm not going anywhere."

My shoulders relax when he goes back on his hunt. This feels familiar. Watching movies with my brother. I walk over to my dresser and rummage until I find an oversized T-shirt I'd stolen from Hudson back in his high school days. It's gigantic and has holes all in it, but Hale is emblazoned across the back and I love it.

I slip into the bathroom to freshen up and make sure I look okay. My eyes seem lighter and glisten with happiness. I'm unfamiliar with the eyes staring back at me. I like these eyes, though. I'd love to see more of them. Reaching behind me, I unzip the dress and let it fall to the floor. My nipple is still red from where he nipped at it. I want him to bite me everywhere.

The burn on my ribs from my new tattoo isn't nearly as bad as I'd expected. His handwriting is permanently etched on my flesh and it's beautiful. I can't wait until I can take the bandages off to properly look at it. The fact he has a matching one makes my heart sing.

We can't have that. Sex. The final step in uniting two people who are in love.

But we can have this.

Us.

Three quarters of a whole, but still more satisfying and fulfilling than anything I could ever hope to have. Kisses and touches and love in secret, even without consummating said love with the act of sex, are enough. More than I could have ever dreamed of having months ago.

I pull on the worn T-shirt and messily tie my hair up in a top bun. When I come out of the bathroom, Hudson's giant body is sprawled out on my bed. He's wearing a pair of old sweatpants that sit low on his hips, accentuating the way his lower abdomen muscles veer down into a perfect V shape. Because he works out so much for baseball, his stomach seems to be carved from stone. Perfect and tanned. His pecs are sculpted and it makes me thirsty for a lick of his nipples too. Between his pecs is a smattering of dark hair that's slightly darker than what's on his head and matches perfectly with the trail that starts below his naval and dips under the waistband of his sweats. The bandage on his side makes my heart patter in my chest.

He's mine.

Secretly so.

Still mine.

"Kill the lights and get in bed," he instructs, like the bossy big brother I know and love.

I roll my eyes, but a smile tilts my lips up. It's not necessary since we're alone, but I'm desperate to keep our secret just that, so I close the bedroom door and lock it before turning off the lights. By the time I slide into bed, he's started a movie. As though my body was made to mold to his, I curl up against him and he wraps an arm around me, pulling me closer. Cuddling with him relaxes me.

"What's this?" he teases as he tugs at the hem of my shirt. "I threw this out years ago."

"I wanted it."

He chuckles. "Looks better on you anyway." His fingers drag the material up over my hips and expose my panties to him, but he doesn't look. "Watch the movie, Rylie."

"Stop distracting me then," I grumble, my palm rubbing against his washboard abs. The movie is the last thing on my mind. In fact, I haven't even looked at the television because I'm fascinated by the way his cock hardens in his sweats, tenting the fabric, just from my touching his stomach.

"Watch the movie," he hisses when my hand slides lower.

"I'd rather watch you."

My palm pushes beneath his waistband and I grip his thickness. It's hot and jolts in my hand, making me smile. "*This* is okay," I tell him, "because it isn't *that.*"

His breath hitches. "*This* feels good, baby."

"Pull your pants down and let me see it," I breathe.

I expect him to argue, but he uses one hand to jerk them down, freeing him to me. My hand seems small wrapped around his large girth. I've watched enough porn to know Hudson is well-endowed in the lower region. Not only is his cock incredibly thick, but he's long too. I'm jealous that Amy had him before. And the girl he let suck him off when he cheated on her.

"I don't want you to be with any other girls," I tell him, the jealousy making the words come out bitter. I don't stop my stroking. I'm eager to make him feel good.

"I don't want to be with any other girls, Ry. I want to be with you."

I can't help myself, so I probe further. "You wanted to be with Amy at one time."

He reaches over and cups my cheek, turning my head to look at him. Green eyes bore into mine. "The way I wanted Amy doesn't even compare to the way my soul fucking needs you. Do you understand that? She was teenage infatuation I thought I had to follow through with. Mom knew what she was talking about there. But you? I need you more and more each second. Thinking of that motherfucker, Travis, even looking at you makes me want to kill him. The idea of you having sex with anyone makes me blind with rage. It's not fucking fair."

He kisses me hard as his palms find my hips. I'm dragged across his waist so I'm straddling him. I moan when he squeezes my ass with both hands. "I changed my mind," he says, chuckling against my lips. "I don't like this shirt."

I giggle when he practically rips it off me. Once he tosses it away, he cups both of my breasts. His cock jolts between us. It's mashed against his stomach. Rocking my hips, I rub against his length. My panties are soaked and I wonder if he can feel it.

"We could," I whisper.

"We won't," he growls. "Rylie, I'm serious. I'll never be able to fuck you. This will have to be enough for us. If we did and anyone found out, we'd be torn apart. For years and years. Who knows how long." He pinches my nipples and tugs them. "I can't lose you. You're the only family I have left that I give a damn about. We have to be smart or it'll all be taken away."

"I will never tell a soul. Even if they tried to torture the truth from me," I vow.

"Same, heathen. I will lie until the day I die."

"If all I can have is this—a tiny piece of fabric separating me from how I fully want you—then that's what I'll take."

He grins at me. "It'll be enough. Most people in this life strive for this and never come close to the feelings we have. I was in a serious relationship. Sex was involved, but it paled in comparison. Not having sex with you but still having you like this is more than I could have ever hoped for."

His palms slide down to my waist and then he uses his thumbs to drag my panties toward the crack of my ass, giving me a royal wedgie.

"Hey," I grumble.

He laughs. "Trust me. You trust me, right?"

"You know I do."

"This will be as close as I can get us," he murmurs, his voice husky. He moves his hands to my front. Gently, he pulls my panties between my outer pussy lips. Then, he grabs my hips and guides me to rub against his cock. My sensitive skin slides along his and I can feel him like I've desperately wanted to.

"Oh," I whisper. "I like this."

"Your panties are so wet. Your cunt is so smooth. I thought you couldn't shave." His fingers dig into my hips and I know I'll bruise. I like the idea of him marking me.

"She monitors it by sitting in the bathroom while I shower, but at least I can shave," I explain, my voice shaking with need.

"You feel good, Rylie. Come here."

Leaning forward, I kiss his full lips. I control our kiss while he manages the way our bodies rub together. My clit may be hidden behind my panties, but he thrusts against it in a way that has me seeing stars.

"I could come just like this," I breathe.

He bites my lip and tugs. "In another world, I'd push my cock inside your tiny cunt. I'd ruin you for any other man."

"You already have."

"I bet your pussy would cream all over my cock as I stretched you to the point of pain. You're so little that I'd bruise your insides, baby. I'd fucking hurt you."

"I want you to hurt me," I moan. "Please."

"Don't beg for shit I can't deliver, heathen. It's too goddamned tempting."

"I'd go to prison for you," I tell him stubbornly.

"I'd die before I let that happen."

"Your finger isn't against the law, is it?" I ask.

He groans. "Rylie."

"It's just a finger. Nobody has to know."

I expect him to deny me, but he slips a finger past my

panties that are bunched between my pussy lips and prods the sensitive flesh.

"There," I breathe. "Right there."

Gently, he urges a finger inside of me like I've done many times before. My fantasies could never compare to the reality of it. The way he expertly knows how to move inside me. It took me years to discover what felt good and it's as though he was born knowing how to do it.

"Hudson," I beg. "Please."

"What are you begging for?"

"More."

"You can't have my fat cock, but I'll fill you up." He pushes another finger inside me. It hurts, but it also feels good. When he curls them and starts rubbing a sensitive spot within me, I cry out in pleasure. "That's it, heathen. I'm going to make you come by touching you right there." He emphasizes his point by pressing against me there. I jolt and squirm. His hand that's still on my hip tightens to keep me still as he continues his ministrations inside me. "Ride my hand, baby."

Shamelessly, I rock against his hand, working with him to bring me to unknown pleasure. As I begin to lose control, I grow needy and desperate. I want it all. I want everything. I want him, consequences be damned. Those thoughts throw me over the edge and I scream out his name as my orgasm bursts through me. I feel too full with his fingers inside me. He never stops his rubbing, even as I climax, and it seems to draw it out longer than ever before. All I can do is tremble violently.

"Show me what I can't have," he barks, his voice raspy with desire.

I lift on my knees despite how shaky I am as he slides his

fingers from me. He pulls my panties to the side and stares at my pussy as though it holds life's answers for him. His tongue darts out and he licks his bottom lip.

"Fucking beautiful," he praises. "I want to stretch this little pussy wide-open with my cock, baby. I want to fill you up with so much cum it would drip out of you for days."

"So do it," I beg.

His jaw clenches, but he does no more than admire what he thinks he can't have. I grip his big dick and slide it against my opening that drips with my orgasm. The tip of his dick presses into me, but he's too big. I stare at him helplessly.

"Rylie," he bites out, his face contorted in rage.

"Hudson, please," I choke out.

"We can't…"

Time seems to stop. He's not fighting me as I clumsily try to get him deeper inside me. I fail miserably.

"I want us to have this," I cry out in exasperation. "But… it won't fit…"

His eyes flicker with madness and fire. He loses control. "It'll fit, goddammit." With those words, he grips my hips and pushes me down along his shaft at the same time he thrusts his hips up hard.

I scream because it's painful and feels as though he's ripping me in two, but the scream is also a battle cry. We've finally won this war. I'm useless, but he doesn't seem deterred. With ease, he rolls us on the bed so he's on top. His hips thunder against me again, sending more exploding pain rippling through me. Tears leak from my eyes, but I'm happy. So damn happy. He's lost to the sickness. His teeth bite my throat almost painfully as he fucks me. Between his bites, he's sucking the flesh and touching me everywhere he can get his hands. All I can do is claw at him and beg for him to never let me go.

He doesn't let go.

If anything, he holds me tighter.

A guttural sound rips from him and then he's coming. His heat floods inside me, burning me from the inside out. It seals and binds us. We're one now, I can feel it. The moment his cock stops twitching, he collapses on me, crushing me to the mattress. His strong arms slide beneath me and he hugs me hard enough that it feels like he might break me.

"What have we done?" he whispers.

I drag my fingertips across his muscled back and kiss his hair. "We found a cure. We're not sick anymore," I tell him. "Don't you feel it?"

He lifts up and regards me with manic eyes. "We're not sick."

"Not sick," I agree.

His body relaxes and it makes his softened cock slide out of my sore body. Cum gushes out of me and slides down my crack. "Nobody has to know."

"Only us."

He smiles and kisses my mouth. "Only us."

SEVENTEEN

Hudson

I wake to the sound of thunder. It takes me a moment to realize I'm not dreaming. Last night, I fucked my sister. And I've never been happier. Regret isn't a feeling that takes space in my mind. Fear, however, does. If anyone ever finds out...

I'm not sure I can live with what would happen to her. I can take care of myself, but with Rylie, she doesn't deserve anything bad to come her way. Her naked, spent body is sprawled out beside me. At some point in the middle of the night, she rolled onto her stomach and looks so damn cute as she sleeps. The room remains fairly dark, but I can make out her features easily enough. Dark lashes fan down over her high cheekbones. I can't see her freckles on her nose in the dim light, but I know they're there. What I become fixated on, though, are her lips. Pink and plump and perfect.

My cock is erect and ready to play, but I'm not sure how she'll feel this morning. Maybe she'll have regrets. If she does, I'll respect that. I love her and don't want her to feel as though she's made a mistake. It feels anything but a mistake for me. It feels like I finally did something right and for me. No more pleasing parents or coaches or teammates or girlfriends I didn't love. Having Rylie is pure selfishness. I've given in to the thing I want most in the world.

And it feels fucking amazing.

I roll her over onto her back and kiss her bare breasts. It starts out innocent enough, but then I'm sucking and biting. Her moans and sharp breaths indicate she's woken up. When her fingers thread into my hair, it's the only encouragement I need. I make it my sole purpose to put as many love bites on her flesh as I can.

"I thought maybe you'd wake up and regret last night," she says, her voice husky from sleep.

I release her skin from my teeth and frown. "Do you regret last night?"

"Hell no."

"I don't either. I want more." I kiss down her stomach to her navel. "I told you that if I ever had you, I'd become crazed. I warned you, Rylie."

She chuckles. "About time you got down to my level."

I nip at her skin and she gasps. Pushing apart her thighs, I open her cunt up to me. Even in the dim lighting, I can tell it's still red from taking a beating last night. She lets out a moan when I kiss her clit. Her scent is one that gets burned into my memory. I want to imbed it in my brain so I never forget.

"Are you sore?" I ask before running my tongue along her slit.

She jerks on the bed. "Y-Yes."

"Want me to stop?"

"Never."

Using my thumbs, I pull her pussy lips apart, exposing her tender pink hidden flesh. Fucking beautiful. I tease her clit with the tip of my tongue until she's writhing and yanking at my hair. When I suck on her clit, her knees try to come together, but I push her back apart as I ravish her cunt.

"Oh God," she cries out. Her body jolts and spasms as

I draw out an orgasm from her simply using my tongue. "I need you."

I kiss my way up her body and latch my teeth on her neck. I give her a painful tug before I pull away. "Your little cunt is too sore."

She huffs. "I don't care. I want you, Huds. You're going to leave Monday and I'm greedy for every second with you."

I rub my dick against her clit. "Are you sure?"

"Yes."

Gripping my cock, I tease her slippery opening before pushing gently into her. She grits her teeth but doesn't make a sound of protest as I slide all the way into her. Her body is so fucking tight. I already have the urge to come and I'm barely inside her. Bare.

"Last night we were reckless. I should grab a condom." But I'm not thinking clearly because I make no moves to get up. I slide slowly in and out of her.

"I like feeling all of you."

My dick twitches at her words. "You could get pregnant, Rylie."

A sweet smile tugs at her lips. "Would that be so bad?"

Images of her stomach swollen with our baby—another Hale in this lonely world—is enough to have me no longer going slow. I thrust raggedly, desperate to fill her up. It's probably the worst possible thing that could happen and yet I can't talk myself out of the idea of wanting it. I come with a groan, my cum jetting deep inside my sister.

Careless.

Reckless.

Fucking stupid.

And yet I'm so damn happy.

I slide out of her. My cum leaks from her cunt. Cum

that belongs right where I left it. Using my fingers, I collect what's running out and drag it back up. I push it pack into her pussy that's even redder now that I've fucked it raw.

"It was Travis," she breathes. "I fucked Travis. But he broke up with me."

I glower at her. "What?"

"No one will ever know." Her smile is wicked.

My heart rate slows once I realize what she means. She'll lie to protect me. To protect us.

"I love you, heathen."

She laughs and it's beautiful. My sister has struggled with her depression her entire life. And during a time when she should be suffering the most, on the heels of our parents' deaths, she's thriving. Because of me. Because of what we've become. She was right.

Our love, no matter how sick it seems to others, is a cure.

The rain is relentless, but after a shower this morning—where I fucked my sister against the tile wall—we both agreed to visit our parents' gravesite. I hold the umbrella over her while Rylie squats to place a single yellow rose on each of their headstones. Once she's satisfied, she stands and hugs my middle. The rain patters against the umbrella and soaks through our jeans as it comes down almost sideways. It's chilly and ridiculous to be out here, but we are. And neither of us is in a hurry to leave.

"Their deaths brought us together," she says. "I mean, I was always sick and wishing you were mine. But you? I don't think you would have come to me had they not died."

I scowl and hug her to me. I'd like to think I would have eventually come around to her, but deep down I know the truth. I would have done what was expected, marrying Amy and staying with her out of guilt.

"I'm here now," I murmur, kissing the top of her head. "What do you think Mom and Dad would think about us?"

Rylie sighs. "I don't think they'd approve."

"Mom wanted me to find real love, though."

"True," she admits. "But she would have beat you in the head with your baseball bat if you'd found that love with her baby girl."

Dipping down, I kiss the side of her neck. "The universe dealt us a shitty hand, but we figured out a way to win."

She leans back against my chest. "When you finish college next year, let's move far away where no one knows us."

"I like that idea. Definitely not Montana, though."

She shudders and I'm not sure if it's from the cold or from the fact we could go to prison there for the rest of our lives for what we're doing. That's so fucked up. I'd pulled open my laptop earlier and showed her just how important it is for us to keep our relationship a secret.

"Rylie?" I murmur as I slide my hand up to touch the rings on her necklace. "I'm sorry I'm so selfish."

Her hand covers mine. "You're not selfish."

"I should have let you date and live your life the normal way."

She turns to face me and tilts her head up, her brows furrowed together angrily. "I was never happy, Hudson. Never. The moment things started crackling between us, I found hope. When we crossed the line with touches and kisses, I was terrified you'd think it was a mistake. Now that we've made love, I'm truly happy. I don't want normal. I want you."

I kiss her mouth. "You have me. You'll *always* have me because I'll never fucking let you go."

~♀~

"I love this part," Rylie says, talking about the movie.

My hand is under her hoodie and I'm palming her breast. I suck on her neck, no doubt bruising her, and laugh. "I love this part too."

After visiting our parents' graves, we changed out of our clothes and decided to watch a movie in the basement since the television is bigger down here. This couch holds fond memories for both of us. Lying beside her, without a care in the world, is the best feeling. Our legs are tangled together. And although we're both wearing lounge pants, our feet are bare. I like rubbing my big feet against her small, soft ones. Truth is, I could spend the rest of my life just lying here cuddling with her. I've never felt so relaxed.

"Where do you want to go eat after the movie?" I ask, squeezing her tit over her bra. My cock is hard in my sweats, but I don't press her for more sex. Holding her is good enough for me.

"You make me eat too much," she complains with a giggle.

I slide my palm to her flat stomach and then tickle her ribs. "You're too damn skinny. I'm going to fatten you up."

She turns and blinks lazily at me. Her pouty lips have parted, begging for a kiss. Leaning forward, I kiss her lips softly at first. But the moment I plunge my tongue into her mouth, she becomes ravenous. A moan tumbles from her and she squirms to twist her body toward me. I slide my palm down the back of her yoga pants under her panties and grab a handful of her ass. She lets out a squeal when I run my finger along her ass crack. We're playfully touching and kissing when we hear it.

A slam.

"Rylie! Hudson!" Aunt Becky's voice is loud as she calls for us upstairs.

As if electrocuted, we both fly apart. Rylie scrambles to one end of the sofa and straightens her hoodie. I pull a pillow from the floor over my erection and attempt to relax on the sofa.

"We're downstairs!" I call out.

Rylie's lips are red from kissing. Fuck.

The door to the basement flies open and footsteps stomp down the stairs. My heart rate is racing, but I manage to stare calmly at the television.

"We're watching a movie if you and Uncle Randy want to join us," I tell her over my shoulder. "It's just barely started."

I can feel Aunt Becky's heated glare on the back of my head.

"Did the retreat suck?" Rylie asks. "I thought you were coming back Monday."

"The speaker ended up getting sick, so we decided to come home and surprise you. Imagine *our* surprise when Hudson's already here. I thought you had a game in Alabama." Aunt Becky's voice is curt and I can hear the accusations she's barely holding back. *I know you two are fucking.*

I peel my eyes from the screen and look at our aunt over my shoulder. She's thin and pretty, her green eyes that look exactly like Mom's blazing with anger. It hurts to look at her sometimes. "Coach benched me."

Her expression softens and her brows furl together.

"Why, Huds?"

"I've been playing shitty. He's pissed."

"It's understandable," she says. "You lost your parents. You'll do better next year."

"Maybe," I mutter.

"Your coach is a dick," Rylie complains. "He doesn't know what it feels like. What we went through."

Aunt Becky lets out a heavy sigh. "Enough of this sad talk. We came back early to celebrate your birthday and that's what we'll do. We're all here together. What do you want to do, sweetheart?"

Rylie turns and grins at me. "I want barbeque."

"Another mud fight?" I tease.

She huffs. "No. There will be no outdoor barbeques, thank you, but there's a place on Main Street I've been wanting to try. They have a mechanical bull," she says with a laugh.

Aunt Becky flinches at her laugh. Like it caught her off guard. It's a reminder that Rylie doesn't normally laugh a lot.

I did this.

I made her well.

We're doing the right thing.

Nobody has to know.

I wink at Rylie. "I smell a challenge."

"Your uncle Randy was a competitive bull rider in high school," Aunt Becky tells us, pride in her tone. "I bet he'll want to be in on this challenge."

"Give me twenty minutes to get ready and it's on," Rylie says, beaming.

I pull the sleeve of my T-shirt up and flex my muscle. "Uncle Randy doesn't have these guns. I'm not falling off that bull."

Aunt Becky laughs. "Oh, please, kid. Randy's held on to me all these years. Sometimes you need more than muscle. You need determination."

I glance over at my sister. "I'm determined, all right."

The four of us are seated at a table and are all laughing. Aunt Becky was right. Uncle Randy's old ass never fell off that bull. I was a close second because muscles do factor in. Rylie fell right off immediately and Aunt Becky never participated. But hearing Rylie's constant giggles has been the real prize for the night. And not just for me. Aunt Becky's bitter face has remained bright and smiling. For a little while, we're able to behave like a family. It reminds me of hanging out with Mom and Dad.

"I've never seen you turn down a margarita," I say to Aunt Becky, observing she's drinking water tonight. Usually at dinner, she at least has wine.

Her smile grows broader and she glances over at Uncle Randy. "Well, we wanted to wait to tell you until we had made it out of the first trimester, but we're pregnant. Finally." She swipes at some tears that leak from her eyes.

"A cousin," I say with a grin.

"This is exciting!" Rylie exclaims. She reaches over and squeezes Aunt Becky's hand. "I'm so happy for you guys."

"We're hoping for a boy," Uncle Randy tells us.

"But we'll be happy with a girl," Aunt Becky quickly amends.

"I'm going to get a job soon as school is out just so I can spoil the baby with lots of clothes," Rylie says.

Aunt Becky smiles. "You don't have to get a job. College is difficult enough without—"

"I'm not going to college," Rylie interrupts.

And just like that, the usual tension between her and Aunt Becky is back.

"Of course you're going to college." Aunt Becky straightens her spine and glowers at my sister.

"I want to go to beauty school like Mom. She loved her job." Rylie fidgets in her seat and I place my palm on her thigh beneath the table, rubbing my thumb across the hem of her dress, letting her know I support whatever she wants to do.

"Don't be ridiculous, Rylie," Aunt Becky snips. "Your mother struggled her entire life to make ends meet. You'll go to college and get a good paying job like Randy and I did."

I want to growl out that Rylie doesn't have to do anything because I'll take care of her, but I bite my tongue. Secrets are secrets because you don't spill them.

"Now's not the time to talk about this," I bite out, cutting this argument short. "It's Rylie's birthday. We're not going to grill her about her future."

I challenge my aunt with a firm stare. Her nostrils flare with fury, but she doesn't say another word.

The food comes and we all chat about easy topics while we have our fill of ribs, baked beans, and homemade macaroni and cheese.

"I'm stuffed," Rylie groans as she pats her nonexistent belly.

"Guess you'll have to dance it off," I tease. "You know how to two step?"

She smirks. "With Lauren Hale as our mother? We

never had an opportunity not to learn how to two step. I think I was dancing long before I could walk."

I rise from my seat and offer my hand. Aunt Becky eyes my palm like it's the head of a venomous snake but again keeps her mouth shut. I feel like deep down, she knows, but she has no proof my dick has been inside her only niece. Uncle Randy is completely oblivious as he nurses his beer.

Rylie gives me her hand and flashes me a playful smile despite the heat blazing in her eyes. I lead her away from the table to the dance floor. Neither of us is a fan of country music, but the whole scene reminds me of Mom and Dad. Even with all Dad's back problems, he'd still get out on the dance floor with her. Lauren and Jerald Hale were made for each other, so much so that they left this world together. Like Romeo and Juliet. I feel like Ry and I are made for each other too. And I'd refuse to live a life without her in it.

I grab onto Rylie's dainty right hand with my left one and hold our clasped hands slightly out to our sides. Then, I hold on to her back just behind her armpit. She extends her left slender arm along over my right one with her palm resting on my shoulder. The song is fast-paced and we quickly start moving to the beat. At first it's uncoordinated, but then we find our rhythm. My eyes never leave her bright brown ones and her smile is all for me. The dance floor is crowded, but we easily maneuver around some older couples doing more complicated routines that require them to stop more. I dance her around the floor over and over, the two of us lost in our own world.

When a slow song comes on, I pull Rylie to a corner behind several other couples and away from Aunt Becky's prying eyes. I hug my sister to me, kiss the top of her head, and rock against her. She relaxes in my hold and lets me control the pace of our slow dance. Despite the rain, she chose a pretty black dress with floral patterns that shows off way too much leg. If we weren't surrounded by people, I'd find a way to work my hands beneath her dress so I could hold on to her ass. Unfortunately, we're not alone and I have to make do with what I have.

Rylie tilts her head up and our mouths are just inches apart. I could kiss her and probably not get caught, but it's too risky. My gaze falls to her lips and I have to ignore the way I want to suck on her bottom one.

"I love you," she says just loud enough I can hear her over the music.

"I love you too, heathen. I wish life were different." My eyes skate over to a couple making out near us. "I wish we had that. Open, free love."

She shakes her head. "I want us. This is enough. What we have is more than enough. I feel lucky we're even allowed that."

I stroke her back. "Now that she's home, I don't know how many free moments we'll get."

She frowns and nods. "I know. We'll find ways. Once I graduate, we'll figure something out."

"I'll spend the entire summer here. Every minute will be with you."

This earns me a beautiful smile. "Come to my room tonight after they go to bed. We can be quiet."

I sneak my hand to her ass and give it a quick squeeze. "You usually scream when I have my cock inside your tiny cunt. It sounds like a bad idea." I wink at her.

She bites her bottom lip and quirks a brow at me. "You could always put something in my mouth to keep me quiet." Then, she purposely rubs her body against my aching cock. "I could be quiet for you."

Lowering my lips to her ear, I tongue her lobe before whispering, "You're a bad girl, Rylie Hale."

"Your bad girl."

For the rest of the night, I can't get the image of silencing my little sister's moans with my fat cock out of my head. Bad, bad girl. I love her, especially when she's bad.

EIGHTEEN

Rylie

My mind is a mess. Not the usual dark and confusing mess. This mess makes perfect sense because Hudson and I are at the center of it. Every thought is of him. The way he makes me feel both emotionally and physically.

"I hope Hudson drives carefully," Aunt Becky says. "The rain is terrible."

I stare out the front windshield as the wipers swipe back and forth frantically. He left early this morning because he has a class this afternoon. Saturday night was fun dancing with him and then Sunday we spent the day watching movies with our aunt and uncle. It was almost as if Aunt Becky knew we wanted to be alone together because she tried to fill up every second by hanging out with us. Thankfully, Hudson did as promised both nights and snuck into my room. We made love many times and as dawn would peek over the horizon, he'd sneak back down to the basement.

I miss him already and he only left a few hours ago.

"He's a good driver and will call us when he gets back," I tell her firmly. I won't allow my mind to get cluttered with images of losing him. He's mine and he's not going anywhere.

As soon as Aunt Becky parks in front of Dr. Livingston's office, I'm irrationally angry. I don't want to come here anymore. I would have thrown a fit and told her I wasn't coming, but Hudson is the one who asked me to go. He was diligent about making me take my medicine all weekend too. I'd like to think I'd be fine, but the way he worries over me melts my heart. I'm doing this for him, not her.

"What? No sigh today?" Aunt Becky teases when she shuts off the car.

I shrug. "It is what it is. Just ready to get this over with so I can go to school."

"School? Since when?" She laughs.

"Since there became an end in sight."

She reaches over and clutches my hand. "I can't believe you're graduating from high school already. Two more weeks and you'll be all grown up. Rylie?"

"Yeah?"

"Just because you don't want to go to college, you're still welcome to stay as long as you like. I don't ever want you to feel like you're pressured to leave our house. You've always got a home with us."

I smile at her but don't tell her my home is with Hudson. "Thanks."

She lets go of my hand and we run through the rain into the clinic. Once I'm settled in a room, alone, I pull out my phone.

Me: I know you're still driving. Be careful. Love you, big brother.

We discussed that our texts can't reveal anything about our relationship in case anyone ever gets a hold of them. It's hard not to say more than what I want, but I can save that for our phone calls.

Hudson: I stopped at McDonalds. So far, so good. Wish I didn't have to go back.

Me: Me too. Two weeks feels like forever. Are you coming to my graduation?

Hudson: I wouldn't miss it for the world.

I grin as I reply.

Me: We need to plan our summer vacation now that Mom and Dad are no longer here.

Hudson: We will. Our traditions don't die with them.

Me: The doctor is about to come in and then I'll be off to school. Text me when you get there so I know you made it safely.

Hudson: Thank you for going. You're doing the right thing. Love you, little sister.

The door opens and I'm forced to put my phone away. Dr. Livingston can't hide his surprise when he sees me.

"Wow," he says, grinning. "Eighteen looks good on you. Smiles look good on you. I take it the medication is working?"

Fucking my brother is helping.

"Yep, I think so."

He sits down in his chair and positions his clipboard on his knee. "I spoke with your aunt. How are things at home?"

I bristle at his words. "Fine. Everything's fine."

Dr. Livingston lifts a brow. "Last time we spoke, you were upset. You were counting down the days until you could move out. What changed?"

Hudson.

"Nothing."

He scribbles something down, his eyes never leaving mine. "Your aunt had some concerns about how much time you've been spending with your brother. She fears you're using him as a crutch. This is a safe place in here. I'm bound to keep what you tell me confidential. You can tell me… anything."

That I'm sleeping with my brother? That's what Aunt Becky has most likely expressed to him as a worry.

He may be bound to secrecy, but I think the area becomes gray when what I say is illegal. I'm not sure he'd keep information like that to himself. It's not his business.

No one will ever know.

"Hudson is my brother and he reminds me I'm not alone in this world. We went to Mom and Dad's graves. Said a few words. It was nice. For the first time, I didn't feel like the world was crushing in around me."

"I see." He waits for me to continue, but I don't. "Besides the medicine, are there certain things or people who make you happy? There's a definite difference in you, Rylie."

He's fishing. He wants me to say Hudson so he can probe more.

"I have a boyfriend," I blurt out. "A guy I met at school. He's in a class of mine." I close my eyes. "We kissed and…" Fucked over and over again. And, oh, he's my brother, not some kid from school. "We've been spending a lot of time together."

"Oh?"

I reopen my eyes and smile. "I love him."

"Love seems like a strong word, especially if this is a new relationship."

Nah, I've known him since birth.

"It's the only word to describe it," I say with a sigh.

"What does Hudson think about this guy?" he asks.

I snort. "He wants to kill him. Hudson doesn't like him, but all big brothers are protective like that."

He chuckles. "I hated all my younger sister's boyfriends. I even hated her husband before she married him. It wasn't until he and I both realized we loved fishing that we became friends. It's natural for your family to feel protective over you. That's how your aunt and uncle feel too. They want to protect you from hurting whether that is self-inflicted or by the influence of others."

"For the first time in ages, I feel truly happy," I tell him honestly. "I'm thankful for my family for worrying over me, but I'll be okay."

"Well, I don't doubt that, Rylie. You've grown up since the last time we spoke. The grief of losing your parents isn't dictating your every thought either. As long as you make good decisions and are being safe, I think you're learning ways to cope and that's never a bad thing. Trial and error is what you have to do. Keep doing what works and eliminate what doesn't work. I'm proud of you."

He continues chatting with me, mainly asking about side effects of my medication and such, but I'm distracted by thoughts of Hudson. He's the best decision I've ever made. I've barely been away from him and I'm already aching to see him again.

Two more weeks, Huds.

"How was your appointment?" he asks, his voice deeper sounding on the phone than in real life.

"Fine. He says I'm doing better. I didn't tell him why."

He chuckles. "I don't think he would have taken that news very well."

"How did class go? Did you even study for your finals?" I question, knowing damn well he didn't crack open a book while visiting me.

"I don't have to study," he gloats. "Besides, they're not

until next week anyway."

"Smug ass."

"What are you wearing?" he teases.

I giggle. "Your hoodie and shorts."

"Where's Aunt Becky?"

"Still at work. It's Monday. She always stays late on Mondays. What are you doing?"

"I was tired as fuck after class because someone kept me awake all weekend, so I came back to my dorm to nap before practice," he says. "But it's raining, so they called practice off. Now, I'm just lying here in my boxers all alone."

I groan as I slide under my covers. "I wish I were there. I'd keep you company."

"That sweet voice of yours makes me hard as fuck," he hisses. "My dick still smells like you. It sucks I have to jack myself off when all I can think about is being deep inside of you."

"Hudson," I breathe as I push my fingers under my shorts and panties to seek my clit. "Why do you have to talk so dirty? Now my clit is throbbing. That was mean."

His chuckles turn me on. "You miss my tongue, heathen?"

"More than anything."

"I miss your tongue too. You're a tease with it, but my cock loved it anyway."

We both grow quiet, both of us panting as we touch ourselves. My orgasm teases me, but it's much harder to do it on my own. He knows exactly how to touch me to make it happen so quickly.

"Fuck, baby, I miss you so goddamned much already. This is torture," he hisses.

Tears burn at my eyes. "I miss you too." My fingers

fumble at my clit, but it's no use. It's not the same. He grunts and then lets out a ragged sigh as he comes. The sounds coming from him lack their usual passion.

"It's no comparison to the real thing," he utters.

"What the fuck, man? Coach cancels practice and you have phone sex with your girlfriend? Hi, Amy," his friend Nick says in the background.

A spike of jealousy flits through me, but it's better for him to think that way. Hudson plays along with it.

"One day, when you find the girl of your dreams, you'll understand," Hudson grumbles at him.

"I was going to ask you if you wanted to go out tonight, but it looks like you have your hands full. Literally. I'll leave you and Amy alone."

"Knock next time, asshole," Hudson says with a laugh seconds before the door slams in the background. "Sorry about that. You didn't come."

I slide my hand out of my shorts. "I will when I see you next. Only you can make me come so hard I see stars. I'm not as good at it as you."

"Have you thought about where you want to go on vacation?" he asks.

I roll over on my side and stare at the picture of the four of us on our last vacation. We went on our annual trip to Lake of the Ozarks. Mom and I are both wearing big sunglasses and even bigger hats. Dad and Hudson wear matching grins as they hold up their fish they'd caught. It's one of my most favorite places. "To our usual cabin."

"I figured you'd say that. A couple more weeks and we'll get to spend all the time in the world together."

NINETEEN

Hudson

C oach doesn't look up from his computer when I enter his office. His jaw is clenched and he seems tired.

"Sit," he instructs as he swivels in his chair and regards me with a frown.

My stomach hollows out. I can't get it out of my head the time he called me in here to tell me my parents were gone. It replays over and over again in my head.

"What's up?" I ask as I drop heavily into the chair across from him.

"We both know you've played like shit," he says bluntly but not cruelly.

"Yeah," I agree. Especially this week at practice. It's been four days since I left Rylie to come back to school and each day becomes more torturous than the last.

"I'm going to be frank here, Hale," he says with a huff. "Paulson has been picking up the slack and a good fit for third base. He's focused and doesn't make stupid mistakes."

I can't even argue. I've missed balls I'd usually catch and can't hit the ball to save my life. Worst part is, I don't even care. It's as though I'm going through the motions just to pass time.

"Are you kicking me off the team?" I ask, my voice tight.

He pushes an envelope across the desk. "Inside, there's

a letter of recommendation and a check from my wife. She appreciates all you've done for her firm, but she needs someone more reliable working there. Just like I need someone on the team I can count on."

I blink at him in shock. "You're kicking me off the team and firing me?"

His throat bobs as he swallows. "You're not playing anymore this season. I've written you up and you're on watch since your scholarship rides on you playing ball for me. I'm not kicking you off because I know you need this scholarship to go to school. But come the end of summer, you have to try out again. If you're not back to being the Hudson I know, you'll force my hand. I'm sorry. I'd hoped you'd take your finals next week and then go home for the summer. Maybe see someone professionally so you can work through your blinding grief. Then, come back in the fall so we can get your head back in the game. You're one of this school's best players and I hate to see you decline so quickly like this."

I keep waiting for the horror to wash over me. Nothing comes. The fact I feel nothing, surprises me. "I'm sorry I disappointed you," I say, my voice husky as I rise from my seat. "I'm going to find myself this summer." It's a long time coming. With Rylie, I've barely begun to scratch the surface.

He lets out a heavy breath. "Find it quickly. You can't afford to screw up your future over a few hard months."

I shake my head at him. "I don't think I'll suddenly get over the death of my parents and how it affects me by August. Just warning you."

"You know what I mean," he grumbles. "If you don't get your head out of your ass, you'll be gone. You need to understand that, Hale."

"I get it, Coach." With that, I slip out of his office and walk over to the bench where Nick is changing.

"What did Coach want?" he asks.

"He gave me an ultimatum."

"What the fuck, man?"

"I'm done for the rest of the season."

"What do you mean done?" he asks, his brows furling together.

"Like done. I won't be practicing or playing. I can try out for the team before next semester starts."

He gapes at me in horror. "No. That's fucked up. Baseball is your life."

No, it was my life.

Now, everything revolves around her.

I simply shrug. "Not anymore."

As I walk out of the locker room, a weight lifts from my shoulders. I may not feel the same later, but at this point, I only feel relief. I quickly text Rylie the news.

Me: I'm off the team for the rest of the summer and I no longer have a job.

But at least I have you.

I don't text her that part in case Aunt Becky is tracking our messages.

Rylie: Oh, Hudson. I'm sorry.

Her simple text is enough. It's more than enough. I don't care about all the things I once cared about.

All I care about is her.

⸱♡⸱

I wake when someone pulls my textbook off my face. After not only getting kicked off the team but also getting fired, I came back to my dorm room to at least study for my finals. I may be slacking off in other areas, but I'll be damned if I fail my exams. But apparently I'm not too worried about studying because I passed the fuck out.

"Shouldn't you be on the field kissing Coach's ass?" I grumble to Nick, squinting against the light.

"I'd rather be kissing you."

Rylie.

She's standing in my room looking fucking perfect.

"Come here, heathen," I demand as I sit up.

She launches herself into my arms and her lips fuse to mine. I grab her ass, pulling her to straddle me. When she's right where I want her, I break our kiss to look at her. Her plump lips are wet and swollen from our needy kiss. Wide brown eyes dart back and forth as she assesses me. Her brows are scrunched together in concern.

"You came to see me," I murmur, my chest thumping with happiness.

She smiles and runs her fingers through my hair. "You had a bad day. How could I not come see you?"

We kiss again. I've missed her hot tongue in my mouth and the way her body melds perfectly to mine.

"I missed you so much," I tell her, my voice cracking.

She swallows and her eyes grow teary. "I missed you too."

"How did you get here?"

"Aunt Becky let me borrow her car."

I frown in confusion. "To come see me? I'm surprised she'd allow that. We both know she's onto us, baby."

Her grin is wicked. "I told her I wanted to go floating down the river with Travis and some friends."

A spike of jealousy at hearing his name is quickly

doused because that means she's mine all weekend. "Thank you."

Our lips press together and my palms roam all over her, desperate to touch everything I've been craving since Monday morning.

"Nobody but Nick and the team knows you're my sister. As long as we go somewhere away from campus, we don't have to hide," I tell her, grinning.

"I like hiding with you." Her eyes twinkle with happiness.

I glance over at the clock. Nick won't be back for at least two more hours. Plenty of time. Gripping the bottom of her dress, I slide it up her thighs and past her hips. She raises her arms over her head to assist me. Once her dress is gone and I have a perfect view of her perky tits in her black bra, I'm in heaven. Fuck, how I've missed her.

Leaning forward, I nip at her tit through her lacy bra. She whimpers but then frantically starts yanking at my shirt.

"Take your bra off and show me your pretty tits, Rylie," I instruct.

She reaches behind her, her hooded eyes boring into me, and undoes her bra. It hits the floor. Her nipples are hard and peaked, eager to be sucked on. I grab a handful of her breast and run the tip of my tongue in circles around her nipple. Then, I suck the small bud into my mouth. I pop off of her and then look up at her.

"I can't take being away from you," she whispers. "Tell me you feel the same. Tell me I'm not crazy."

I lean closer and gently bite her now red nipple. "I go fucking crazy without you too."

She lets out a relieved sigh. "Another week and then we can spend every moment together."

I slip my fingers between us and rub her clit over her panties. "Every moment," I vow, my voice low and desperate. "I'm going to find us a place together. Everything is going to work. It has to."

"It will," she agrees. "As long as we're together, it'll work."

She lets out a moan when I pick up my pace rubbing her. Her hips rock back and forth, eager for my touch. I love how wet her panties are. She's just as needy for me as I am her.

"Hudson," she breathes, her body jerking as pleasure starts taking over. "Oh, God."

"That's it," I growl. "I want you to come and soak these panties. I've missed you, dirty girl. Show me just how dirty you are."

She cries out and her head tilts back, exposing her neck to me. I nip at her collarbone as I draw a much-needed orgasm from her. My sweet girl comes hard and loudly. The moment she comes down from her high, I twist us around and lay her back on my bed. Her gaze is heated as I pull her drenched panties down her thighs and toss them away. As soon as she's naked, I stand and lose the rest of my clothes.

"You're so perfect," I praise as I crawl over her body.

We're like two magnets. When we get near one another, we naturally gravitate toward the other and fit perfectly together.

I grip my aching cock and rub the tip along her slit. She's slick with arousal, so I'm easily able to push into her tight cunt. We both let out relieved grunts. I thrust my hips and drive the rest of the way in, earning a strangled cry from her.

"Kiss me," she begs.

My lips crash to hers as she claws at me in desperation. Neither of us can get enough. I want to breathe her into my motherfucking soul and keep her there.

"Hudson," she moans.

I buck my hips hard. Pleasure buzzes through my every nerve ending. Our tongues thrash together wildly. I suck on her lip. Then, she bites mine.

"Fuck, I won't last long," I groan. "You feel too good. I can't fucking control myself around you."

"Come," she purrs. "Come inside me. I like the way it feels. Like you're claiming me."

Her words madden me. Fuck yes, I've claimed her. She's mine. No matter what any asshole on this planet has to say about it.

Fuck the rules.

Fuck the law.

Fuck society.

I'm going to fuck my sister because I love her and she loves me.

"I'm going to make you come again first," I tell her as I seek out her clit once more. She jolts when I connect with the sensitive nub. "Does that feel good, heathen? When I have more time with you, I want to suck on it until you cry and beg me to stop."

"Hudson," she whimpers. "Too much…"

"Not enough. Never enough."

Her orgasm hits her violently, causing her back to arch up off the bed and her pussy to clench around my cock. It sends me off the rails. My climax rips through me hot and furious. As my dick throbs my release into her, I collapse against her and devour her mouth.

We kiss until I've long since turned soft and my cum

runs from her spent body.

"What's so wrong about our love?" she asks when I finally pull away from her mouth.

I stroke some strands of hair from her face. "Nothing."

She sighs. "They think it's wrong."

"And they don't know shit."

"Seriously, though. I want to know who came up with these rules. I don't understand." Her nose scrunches in confusion. "Back in the medieval times, people married their relatives all the time to keep the bloodlines pure. When did it stop being acceptable?"

I kiss her nose. "I don't know."

"It's stupid."

"But it's the law. And if anyone finds out…" I swallow, unable to finish that thought. I'm proud as fuck to have her as my girl. But I'm scared as hell about what would happen if anyone found out. "They can't find out."

"I'd die before I spent the rest of my life without you, Hudson."

Sweet, beautiful girl.

"I sure as hell wouldn't want this life without you either."

She smiles. "Like Romeo and Juliet."

"Why does our love story have to be a tragedy?"

Tears well in her eyes. "Mom and Dad's love story was a tragedy. I guess all the good ones are."

"Not ours, baby. Ours won't be a tragedy."

"Promise?"

"Promise."

TWENTY

Rylie

"Burgers or pizza?" Hudson asks as he hunts for his shoes.

I pull my dress into place and pat down my messy hair. "Hmmm. Burgers sound good."

He stops looking for his shoes to walk over to me. His arm hooks around my waist and he pulls me to him. "I'm glad you're eating. It makes me happy."

I smile shyly at him. "You make me hungry."

His grin is boyish but kind of wicked too. "You make me hungry too."

We both laugh but then his mouth is pressed to mine again. Even though my stomach has been growling, I could go for another round. Our twenty-minute break where we cuddled quietly was enough to recharge us both. His palms squeeze my ass through my dress. My breath hitches when he starts sliding the fabric up again.

The door bursts open and we both jerk apart. His friend Nick takes in the scene and his goofy grin falls.

"Did I interrupt something?" His brows furl together. "Rylie?"

I give him a little wave. "Hey."

He turns an accusing glare to Hudson. Before he can open his mouth, Hudson takes a step toward him, his shoulders tense. The testosterone in the room is suddenly thick and palpable as Hudson silently challenges Nick to say something.

"We were going to grab burgers if you're hungry," I chirp, hoping to distract him.

"Uh, right," Nick says, stepping back. "Burgers sound good. Jada and Caitlin invited a bunch of us to the lake again."

I wince at hearing Jada's name.

"I think we'll pass," Hudson says, sensing my unease.

"I think you should go," Nick bites out, his gaze darting my way.

He knows. Just like Aunt Becky knows. I can feel it.

"We'll go. I was just trying to console Hudson. He's had a bad day. That's what sisters are for." I beam, hoping to convince him I'm merely doing my sisterly duty. "We'll go."

Nick, clearly smarter than he looks, glances over at the disheveled sheets and the discarded towel Hudson used to clean us up with. The room smells like sex, no denying it.

"Right," he utters, his lip curling up slightly as if he's disgusted. "Probably a good idea."

Hudson looks over his shoulder at me and I flash him an encouraging smile. A smile that says we need to do this to show him we're simply a normal brother and sister who aren't fucking.

"Fine," Hudson agrees.

Nick gives a slight shake to his head but says nothing else before stalking out of the room.

So much for being careful.

By the time we make it to the lake, it's dark out. About

twenty vehicles are parked at a clearing near the water. People are laughing and drinking near a bonfire. During dinner, Hudson and I played it safe. Eventually, Nick calmed back down. I think we've convinced him because he goes back to being his usual jokester self. Hudson is stiff but forces himself to joke around with Nick as though our secret isn't a thick fog hanging around us.

"Nick!" a girl yells as she runs our way. She throws herself into his arms and kisses him. The girl is drunk already.

"Hey, Caitlin. Missed you, beautiful," he says, his hands on her ass as he carries her off.

Hudson and I exchange relieved looks.

"Long time, no see, stranger," a sultry voice says from behind us.

I turn to see a pretty blonde walking our way.

"Jada," Hudson greets.

My entire body grows tense as I wilt in her presence. She's prettier, has much bigger breasts, and has had my brother's dick in her mouth. I'm jealous and hate her. No denying that.

"I'm Jada," she says, extending her hand to me.

"I'm Hudson's…" I pause. "Sister."

Her eyes widen. "So nice to meet you. For a second, I thought you were Amy." A giggle escapes her, making her boobs bounce with the movement. It makes me want to drag Hudson far away from this woman.

I shake her hand despite not wanting to. "Nope. Just Rylie."

"Rylie came to visit," Hudson says as his palm rubs up and down my back. "If you don't mind, we're going to find someplace quiet to talk. Things are hard since losing Mom and Dad."

Her brows scrunch together. "Of course. I'm so sorry for what you're both going through."

I give her a pleasant smile but then let out a breath of relieved air when she walks off.

"I hate her," I hiss under my breath.

Hudson shoots me a hot look. One that says, *You have nothing to worry about because it was you I was inside a couple of hours ago.* "Come on."

I follow him to where someone has a big water cooler sitting on the back of a tailgate. Something tells me it's not filled with water, though. Hudson pulls two Red Solo cups from a bag and sets to filling us up on the mystery liquid. He hands me my cup and I take a sip.

"Tangy," I say and shudder. "And strong."

"Don't drink too much, lightweight."

A couple of guys walk over to us. We spend the next hour chatting and hanging out. One can't keep his eyes off me, though. As they talk about baseball, I find that Hudson has moved to stand almost completely in front of me.

"Find something interesting?" Hudson snaps, interrupting the one named Brian to glower at the one beside him. The one who keeps staring at me I've learned is Logan.

"You don't have to hide," Logan says, grinning at me. "I don't bite."

"Don't talk to my sister." Hudson is tense and after several glasses of the mystery punch, he's feeling the effects of the alcohol and is poised for a fight.

"Hudson," I murmur and clutch onto his T-shirt from behind.

Logan chuckles. "Protective older brother. I get it. I won't hurt her. Just wanted to get to know her."

"No," Hudson barks.

I flash Logan an apologetic look, but he smiles, unde-terred. Great. Wisely, he only chooses to check me out when Hudson isn't paying attention. Feeling uncomfortable, I take to sucking down my drink. Everything is becoming blurry around me.

"Nick says everyone has to get naked and in the lake," Jada says as she approaches. She peels off her shirt, baring her breasts to our little group. Brian curses in appreciation and Logan starts tugging off his own shirt.

Jada's eyes are for my brother only as she seductively starts pulling down her shorts. Hudson turns to look at me. "We're not going skinny-dipping. Not with that asshole eye-fucking you every second."

"Hey, Rylie," Logan calls out to me as he drops his shorts. I get an eyeful of his junk before I quickly look back up at Hudson.

Hudson's jaw is clenched and he's seething with fury. "I'm going to kill him."

Discreetly, I grab his wrist. "It's fine. Let's do this. We're supposed to not be attracting attention to ourselves."

I step away from him and pull my dress off. Hudson's stare is predatory as he watches me undress. I'm not confi-dent being that Jada and her porn star tits are only a few feet away. Thankfully, Brian tosses her naked ass over his shoul-der and runs out to the lake with her. It leaves Logan, proud and naked, to loiter nearby.

"It'll be fine," I whisper. "Now get naked and stay close."

He yanks off his shirt and then pushes off his shorts. His cock is erect as his gaze roams hungrily over my nearly na-ked body. With shaking fingers, I take off my bra and pant-ies. Logan lets out an appreciative whistle.

Hudson cracks his neck and if I don't get him into the

water soon, he's going to kill Logan.

"Race you," I tell them both before taking off running.

By the time I reach the lake, I see nearly everyone already out in the water. People are squealing and laughing and having a good time. I splash into the water and then dunk myself. It's cold and my nipples harden immediately. Logan and Hudson both make a beeline for me. Where Logan's gaze is playful and flirtatious, Hudson's is manic and furious. I want to crawl into Hudson's arms and tell him to calm down. To kiss him until he does.

Jada wades over to us and stands so that her big tits are out of the water for all to see. I remain under the water to my chin. I'm not even close to looking as good as she does naked. So I hide. Logan inches closer.

"How old are you? You're not jailbait, are you?" Logan teases.

A possessive palm grips my ass and I flash Hudson a shy smile. "I just turned eighteen last week."

Logan grins. "Then you're most definitely my type."

"I have a boyfriend," I blurt out.

Hudson squeezes my ass.

"I have a girlfriend," Logan throws back at me. "What she doesn't know won't hurt her."

"Speaking of girlfriends," Jada says, her voice sultry as she regards my brother. "Are you still with Amy? We could always pick up where we left off last time." She comes to stand close to him, her boobs brushing against his muscular arm.

"I'm seeing someone new," Hudson says. "I love her. I'm going to marry her." The fierce bite in his voice leaves no room for argument. Jada opens her mouth but then wisely swims over to Brian and starts flirting with him.

Logan takes a deep breath and sinks under the water. For a moment, we're alone. Hudson's palm on my ass is comforting. It's discreet, but we both need the touch. Something grabs me by the ankle and I scream before I'm taken under.

Logan!

He drags me away beneath the surface, his palms greedily groping me. I thrash back to the top and gasp for air, frantically searching for Hudson. I hear Logan gasp for air behind me before his strong arms lock around my middle. Back down into the water we go. His cock is hard pressed against the crack of my ass. Panic surges through me as I worry what he'll do. Surely he wouldn't. But then he's poking at me with it.

No!

I scream and thrash as I fight to break the surface again. People are laughing thinking we're playing. Just as Logan's arms go around me again, he's ripped away from me. In the moonlight, Hudson's face is positively murderous. He grips Logan by the throat in his left hand and starts pummeling the hell out of him.

Punch. Punch. Punch.

His arm is poised for another hit when Nick and Brian pull them apart. Logan's nose bleeds and he glowers at Hudson. "What the fuck, man?"

"Nobody touches her," my brother hisses. "She's my little sister."

"Get her out of here," Nick growls, disgust dripping from his tone.

Hudson grips my wrist and starts hauling me from the lake. As soon as we're standing on the banks, he drags me past the bonfire. We scoop up our clothes along the way and then I'm hurrying to keep up with him as he weaves between parked cars as he looks for his truck. Once we reach it, he throws his stuff into the back and then does the same with mine.

"Did he hurt you?" he demands, his palms sliding to my cheeks. He tilts my head up so he can look at me.

"No," I assure him. "He was rubbing himself against me and it freaked me out."

"I'm going to fucking kill him," he roars and starts back toward the lake.

Dripping wet with fury gleaming in his eyes, he looks like a monster. A monster that would destroy someone like Logan. I can't let him do that because they'll take him to jail. I need him.

I grip at his shoulders and then latch onto his neck. "Don't leave me."

His eyes, hot with anger, drop to my lips. I lick them to entice him. A growl resounds from him before he attacks my mouth. The violence of his kiss nearly knocks me off my feet. When my knees buckle, he hooks an arm around my waist and walks me back to the truck. My breasts are pressed against his muscled chest and his hard cock throbs between us.

He yanks the door to his truck open, using it as a shield to hide us and then he breaks our kiss. "Bend over," he orders.

I bite my lip but turn around to obey him. With my body folded over his seat and my ass prone to him with people not far away, I feel completely vulnerable. My pussy is slick with want and I wiggle my ass, eager for him to fuck me.

With one hand, he fists my wet hair. Using the other

one, he guides his cock into me. I cry out when he tugs my hair so I'm fully standing. From this position, I feel completely full of him and at his mercy. His hand slides around to my front and massages my clit as he thrusts into me from behind.

"Unh! Unh! Unh!" My sounds are feral and uncontrolled. I know I should be quiet, but I can't. Not when he fucks me like it could be the last. As my orgasm nears, my legs begin shaking wildly. "Unh! Unh!" Our bodies are still wet from the water and slap together noisily.

Someone could see.

Someone could hear.

"You're fucking mine," he hisses against the side of my head.

"Oh—"

His hand slaps over my mouth, stifling my scream as I come. I'm dizzy and losing all sense of reality. Before I'm even done coming down from my high, heat floods into me, marking me from the inside.

Always the best part.

The heat of him surging into me.

My legs keep buckling, but he never lets me go. His cock slides out of me and then he eases me down to rest on the seat. The moment his heat is gone from behind me, I choke on a sob. I want him close. I need his comfort.

"Here, heathen," he says softly. "Let's get you dressed."

He helps me pull my dress on, forgoing my panties and bra. The material sticks to my wet skin, but I'm thankful to be covered from possible onlookers.

"Get inside the truck," he tells me.

I scoot to the middle and he climbs in with me. The door slams shut, but he makes no moves to drive off. He lifts his arm and then tucks me against his chest. Beneath his strong arm, it feels safe and warm. I don't ever want to leave this spot.

"That was careless," he murmurs. "I shouldn't have done that with them so close."

I palm his chest that's now covered in his T-shirt. "But I needed that."

He kisses the top of my head. "I needed that too."

We're silent for a while. The sounds of the other party-goers can be heard not too far away as they laugh and yell.

"It's like I have a fever around you," he admits with a whisper.

"We didn't find a cure," I say as my eyes droop with sleep. "We just got sicker."

TWENTY-ONE

Hudson

The drive back to campus the next morning is awkward. Nick sits in the passenger seat nursing a hangover and keeps shooting glares my way. It's pissing me off. I haven't touched Rylie once during our car ride, no matter how difficult it is not to. Her thigh rubbing against mine is enough to make me lose nearly all focus.

"I need to go grab a change of clothes and then maybe we can go get breakfast," she says cheerily, looking way too beautiful for seven in the morning. Her hair has air dried and is wilder than usual, but her brown eyes are bright and happy. Fuck, she's gorgeous. And mine.

I park close to her car at the school and then climb out. She bounces off and I watch her as she leaves.

"You're fucking your sister."

I snap my head to meet Nick's accusing glare from across the hood of the truck. "Excuse me?"

He rounds the front of the truck with fire gleaming in his eyes. "You're fucking Rylie, you sick fuck."

I stalk over to him and my chest bumps against his. "I'm not fucking my sister, dickhead." I glower down at him. I'm slightly taller and definitely stronger.

"Don't lie to me, Huds," he snarls. "I walked in on you yesterday. The room smelled like your baby sister's pussy."

I shove him hard and he stumbles back. "Talk about my

181

sister again," I threaten. "I fucking dare you."

He stomps back over to me. "You'll go to prison for this shit. They'll rape you in prison for being a sister fucker. They'll—"

I shove him again, this time hard enough his ass hits the pavement.

"Hudson!" Rylie is now behind me and tugs at my arm. "Stop!"

Jerking my head to meet her gaze, I hiss at her. "He's accusing me of fucking you!"

Fear flashes in her eyes and she shakes her head. "W-What? Don't be gross, Nick. You're misunderstanding. Hudson and I wouldn't do that."

Nick gets back to his feet. "I know what I saw. I know what I fucking heard. And I smelled sex!"

I start for him again, but Rylie pushes past me, putting herself between us.

"Nick," she says softly. "You're drunk still and tired. He's my brother. We are not having sex."

His fury melts away as confusion sets in. "But I—"

She clutches his shoulders. I want to pry her hands off him, but I let her handle this. My way of handling it would be smashing his skull in with my fists. "But nothing. I have a boyfriend named Travis. Hudson is on again and off again with Amy. He's protective over me because our parents recently died. Please understand."

He swallows. "Whatever. I'm going to bed."

As soon as he's gone, I point at the truck. "Wait here. I'm getting us a hotel room for the night but need to grab some clothes first."

"Don't antagonize him," she says. "Just get in and get out."

I give her a clipped nod and trot off after my once best friend.

Just get in and get out.

I wake to the sound of an air conditioner humming as it kicks on and it takes me a moment to realize I'm in a hotel room. Rylie's naked body is draped over mine and she snores softly. I stroke her silky hair and wish for a million more moments like this one. Moments where we can freely be together without fear of prying eyes and accusations.

I'm still pissed over Nick.

He has no right to get into my business.

Rylie stirs and lets out a soft moan that speaks straight to my cock. After we left Nick, I booked a hotel room and we spent the rest of the afternoon eating takeout and having sex. My sweet girl is beyond tired and yet my body still craves her, even now. She rolls over onto her stomach, her body all sprawled out. I love what a wild sleeper she is. Sitting up on my elbow, I start pressing kisses along her spine. When I get to the little dip of skin at the base of her back right above the swell of her ass, she twitches.

She's awake.

Good, I want to taste her.

A gasp escapes her when I kiss down the crack of her ass. My tongue is curious and I lick her pussy from behind. Her scent is clean from our shower and I want to dirty her up. I want to smell her arousal. I want to fucking bathe in it. She groans when I grab a handful of her ass and pull it to the side. My nose nudges against her ass as my tongue seeks to plunge inside her cunt.

I playfully nip at her pussy lip. "I want to take every part of you. I want in here one day." A loud moan rips from her when I run my tongue along her puckered hole between her ass cheeks. I let the saliva from my mouth run out and drench her hole as I tease it. Her arousal becomes potent and I can smell it in the air. "You want that," I observe.

She cries out when I grab her hips and pull her with me as I settle onto my back. Her tiny body straddles my face but with her back to me. Gripping her flesh, I encourage her to ride my face. At first, she jerks awkwardly, but then she gets into it. I push my tongue deep into her cunt and smile against her when she starts fucking it as though it's my cock. She leans forward, opening herself up further to me, and then I grunt when her lips close around my dick.

With a growl, I start sucking and licking at her tender flesh. She rocks her hips as she sucks on my cock. Fuck, I'll never grow tired of the way her mouth feels wrapped around me. Her small hand fondles my balls and jolts of pleasure zip through me.

I retract my tongue from inside her and replace it with my thumb. Then, I pull my thumb back out. She whimpers when I probe the tight hole of her ass. I'd love nothing more than to stretch this hole with my fat cock, but she'd fucking cry. She's not ready. It's up to me to get her ready. She trusts me to do so.

"Easy, baby," I murmur against her juicy cunt. "I'm going to work on your ass for a bit. I want to take you here soon."

She moans around my dick, making me grunt. Her body relaxes and I gently urge my thumb into her. It's so fucking tight. In and out, I work her hole. I slip it back out and then push two fingers into her cunt, wetting them. When I pull them out and try for her ass, she clenches her cheeks.

"Let me stretch you," I growl. "Do you trust me?"

"Yes," she breathes and then lowers herself back down on my cock.

I work my middle finger into her nice and slowly. Once I'm sure she's good with that, I pull out slightly and then start working another finger along with it into her. She whimpers and tears drip onto my thighs.

"Relax and it won't hurt," I say, encouraging her.

Her grip on my fingers lessens. "I-I can do this."

I kiss just under her ass cheek as I fuck her tight hole. "Of course you can. You can do anything, baby."

She moans and rocks against my fingers. I want to stretch her with a third, but I won't take it too far without lube. Not tonight. With my fingers in her ass and my tongue inside her cunt, I lose myself to her. She bobs on my length as if it's the only thing in this world she wants to do. I come with a groan. The surprise burst of cum has her gagging.

I slide my tongue from inside her and lap at her clit. It doesn't take her long before she's coming with a shriek. Once she stops shaking, I slip my fingers from her and pop her on the ass.

"Let's get a shower and then I'm taking you out. Nap time is over."

As soon as Rylie emerges from the bathroom after getting ready, I nearly choke on my gum. She's shy as she looks at me from beneath her lashes. There's no reason to be shy, though. She's a goddamned knockout.

The short dress she wears shows off her long legs and I

find myself wanting to skip going to the bar like we'd talked about so no one sees her. Her brown hair has been straightened and hangs down her back, begging to be touched. She's put on makeup and it accentuates her features, especially her plump lips.

"You're trying to kill me," I accuse with a grin as I prowl over to her.

"You look pretty hot yourself." Her smile grows wider.

I grip her hips and pull her against me, my erection hard between us. "I promised you a night out but fuck, heathen, if I don't want to break that promise right now."

She giggles. "I want to go dancing. You can come back and fuck me all night long. But first, dancing."

I kiss her smiling mouth and grab her ass with both hands. "Fine, but I don't know how long I'll last seeing you look so damn hot."

We manage to leave the hotel room without fucking, which was a feat. Once we're outside in the warm spring night, we hold hands, uncaring if these strangers see us together. I walk her along the sidewalk until we come to a restaurant nearby. Music plays and the place is jam-packed.

"Let's eat outside," I tell her as we head inside.

The hostess guides us to a table outdoors and seats us. We get carded when I order us margaritas but thankfully Rylie has her fake ID with her. Minutes later, we're munching on chips and salsa and drinking margaritas.

"You look beautiful." Her eyes light up at my words. I lean forward and tug her necklace out from under her dress so I can admire our rings hanging from her neck. "Better." I wink at her.

"I'm happy, Huds." She beams at me. "Really happy."

"Because you like Mexican food?" I tease.

Her grin grows wider. "Because I can finally have you. It feels right. As long as I have you, I'll always be happy."

I take her hand in mine and squeeze. "Mom and Dad may not have approved of us getting together, but I can't help but think they can feel our happiness wherever they are. I think, deep down, all they ever wanted was our happiness. We've done it, baby. We're both happy."

Her smile falls. "Why does it feel like it could all disappear in an instant?"

Thoughts of sitting inside a cold, empty jail cell flit through my mind. Alone. Without her. That would be fucking hell. "Nobody can ever know."

She nods. "I know."

The rest of dinner goes on fine, but I can't help but look at everyone suspiciously. We even dance a little, but neither of us is into it. Do they know? Once I've paid, I drag her out of the restaurant, eager to get her away from nosy fuckers.

"Where are we going? The hotel is that way," she says, pointing in the opposite direction.

"I want to take you somewhere."

The walk is kind of long but nice. Crickets chirp and I can hear cars on the highway nearby. We approach a small park that's mostly secluded by trees. She's quiet as I open the gate and sneak us inside.

"Let's swing," I tell her.

We settle on the swings but don't do more than sit. Our bodies are twisted so we can face each other.

"Can I see your necklace?"

She nods and unfastens it before handing it to me. I pull the rings from the chain and hand it back to her. Her brows are furrowed with curiosity as she puts the necklace back on.

"I don't know if I'll ever be able to marry you in a church like you deserve," I murmur.

"Hudson…"

I place the bigger ring into the palm of her hand. "But in every sense of the meaning behind the ceremony, I want you in that way. Maybe they won't let us, but our hearts will." I slide the simple band on her ring finger. "If we were allowed, would you want to marry me?"

Tears well in her eyes and she nods. "In a heartbeat."

"Me too, baby. I'm sorry I can't give you what you deserve."

She shakes her head, tears rolling down her cheeks, as she slides my ring on my finger. "You give me everything I want and need. I don't want what everyone else has. I want us."

Leaning forward, I capture her lips with mine. After a long kiss, I pull slightly away and swipe away some wetness on her cheek with my thumb. "I love you more than anything. They'd have to drag me away in cuffs because I'd never willingly leave your side."

Her fingers latch into my hair. "I wouldn't be able to survive without you, nor would I want to."

Our mouths meet again, desperate and hungry. The words we spoke may not be what ones would say in a traditional wedding ceremony, but to us, they're just as binding.

"I love you," she breathes against my mouth. "Only you. Only ever you."

TWENTY-TWO

Rylie

A week later...

"Your parents would be so proud," Aunt Becky says, beaming at me from across the table at the steakhouse where we're celebrating my graduation.

"I'm proud of you," Hudson agrees, winking at me.

My skin grows hot and I have to force myself to look away. Last weekend, after our weekend alone, I had to drive back to finish out my last week of school. Hudson stayed back and completed his finals. Now that I've graduated and his semester is over, a huge weight has been lifted. We haven't been granted alone time yet since he got in this morning, but as soon as Aunt Becky and Uncle Randy go to bed, I'm going to attack my brother.

"Your uncle Randy and I've been looking into cruises. Since your parents aren't here, we thought about taking a family vacation just the four of us before the baby comes. Next summer, we won't be able to," Aunt Becky says.

I deflate at her words. I don't want to vacation with them. I want to go away like Hudson promised me. To our cabin. Alone. Just the two of us.

"The cruise line is one of the best," she continues. "Very expensive but worth every penny. None of those small windowless cabins on this ship."

As she drones on, I can't help but feel sad. When a hand clutches my thigh beneath the table, I dart my gaze to Hudson.

He mouths the word, "No."

I crack a smile. Hudson doesn't break his promises. He told me we'd get the cabin, so we're going to get our old cabin.

"How's Travis?"

Aunt Becky's sudden inquiry into my fake boyfriend has me stuttering. "Oh, uh, he's fine."

She purses her lips and darts her eyes back and forth between Hudson and me.

"Have you talked to Amy lately?" she asks my brother. "I saw her at her shop. She's lost a little weight but is looking great. Asked about you and how you were doing. Wanted me to tell you to call her sometime so you two could catch back up."

"I cheated on her with a chick from college," Hudson bites out, ending Aunt Becky's idealistic dreams of them getting back together. "We're on a break."

"Maybe the break needs to end," she says, her tone curt.

"We're not getting back together." He drains his wine and leans back in his chair, crossing his muscled arms over his chest. The pale blue dress shirt he wore for my graduation molds to his perfect physique. It's hard to keep my eyes off him. He's too hot.

"I see," Aunt Becky says.

"I'm beat," Uncle Randy grunts. "Ready to go back home?"

They pay the bill and the ride home is silent. Uncle Randy, the least talkative of our bunch, holds the entire conversation. We get to hear all about one of his clients and how he nearly beat his golf score. Hudson fumes from beside me and Aunt Becky grinds her teeth loudly. Once we're home, Hudson feigns being tired and leaves us to eat cake alone. Uncle Randy eats his cake quickly and then he escapes.

As soon as he's gone, Aunt Becky says her piece. "Something is going on with you."

I chew the cake and stare at her with wide eyes. "Hmm?"

Her gaze falls to my ring that sits on my necklace once again, not safe to wear on my finger around people. "You and Travis getting serious?"

"Yep," I squeak.

She narrows her eyes. "That's funny because I ran into him today at Amy's store. His mom owns the one next door. When I mentioned you two dating, he laughed."

"He's a jokester," I mutter. "What did he say?"

Her nostrils flare. "He said he wished you were dating."

My cheeks burn under her scrutiny. "He was just messing with you."

"I can tell when you're lying," she snaps, making me jump. "If you two are together, maybe you should get him over here for dinner tomorrow."

"Okay," I hiss. "I didn't know I needed proof of who I was dating."

"Rylie, I'm only trying to help you—"

"I don't need your help," I bite out at her.

꩜

Me: She's such a bitch.
Hudson: I know.
Me: Come see me.
Hudson: Too risky. Come see me.

Me: Give me a few minutes to make sure they're asleep.

I slip out of my bed in the dark and sneak out of my room. The air conditioner keeps the air cold and my bare legs become covered in chill bumps. Hudson will warm me up. I creep over to my aunt and uncle's room and press my ear to the door. Uncle Randy's snores are loud and the television is no longer playing, which means they're both asleep.

Quietly, I make my way down the stairs to the basement door. Then, I sneak downstairs where Hudson stays. The glow from the television illuminates the space. He's not sitting on the sofa but on the floor near some boxes we brought from our old house. His brows are furrowed together and his shoulders are hunched.

"What's wrong?" I whisper as I rush over to him and kneel next to him.

He's holding Mom's baseball T-shirt that says: Hudson's #1 Fan.

"I let her down," he murmurs. He turns his head to regard me and his features are twisted in pain.

"She was always so proud of you." I hug him and kiss the side of his neck. "She'd still be so proud of you. You're more than baseball, Hudson. You're everything to me."

He drops the shirt to run his fingers into my hair. I'm dragged to his lips and he kisses me hard. Our tongues duel for control. He wins. He always wins. I moan against his lips but then he's pulling away all too soon.

"I found something Mom would have wanted you to have," he says as he pulls out a rectangular wooden box.

"Her haircutting scissors." I pluck the box from his hand and open it. The metal glimmers in the light of the television. "Do you remember how pissed Dad was when she bought these?"

"They were nine hundred dollars," he says with a chuckle. "I thought Dad was going to shit a brick."

I smile. "You going to let me practice on your hair?"

His eyebrow arches up playfully, the sad moment long gone. "Are you going to do a good job?" He pulls the box away and sets it onto the carpet beside him. "Or are you going to give me a bowl cut like Mom did when I was in kindergarten? Thank fuck she went to beauty school and learned later what not to do. That was awful."

I swat at him. "Yes, jerk. I'm going to do a good job."

He grips my wrist and tackles me. A giggle escapes me before his hand covers my mouth to keep me quiet. His body is heavy pressed against mine. I can feel every part of him. My thin T-shirt and panties allow me to enjoy every muscle on him. His cock is hard between us and I try to wriggle to get him to rub it against my clit.

"You're a dirty girl, hmmm?" he asks as he slowly grinds against me.

I blink at him and nod. His palm slides from my mouth, dragging my bottom lip down as he makes his way to my jaw. He uses his fingers to open my mouth and then his hand continues down to my throat.

"Hudson," I whisper.

He grips my neck in a possessive way before his lips press to mine. I moan against his kiss, which has him groaning in response. His hand slides down to my breast and he squeezes it over my shirt.

"A week was too long, heathen," he murmurs. "I fucking missed you so much."

"I missed you too. I need you."

His palm slips under my shirt and he runs it along my

bare flesh. I gasp when he pinches my nipple. My panties are wet with need to have him. He drags his palm back down my stomach and digs his fingers beneath my panties.

"These have got to go," he growls.

He starts tugging them when light suddenly floods the basement.

"Fuck," he snaps as he rolls away from me.

I sit up and right my shirt just as Aunt Becky stomps down the stairs and comes into view. Her glare is rage-filled as she takes in the scene.

"I knew it!" she yells, her face turning bright red. "I fucking knew it!"

Hudson rises to his feet, his erection obvious as ever in his sweatpants. Oh God. This is bad. "Knew what?" he challenges, a vein throbbing visibly on the side of his neck.

I scurry to my feet. "We were looking through Mom and Dad's old things and—"

"No!" she bellows. "Stop lying. Just stop the goddamned lying. I know you two are sleeping together. Oh, God." She gags. "What have you done?"

My heart hammers in my chest. "What?! What are you talking about?"

"Stop lying!" she screams.

"Calm the fuck down," Hudson snaps at her, his body naturally moving in front of mine in a protective manner.

"Get away from her!" Aunt Becky yells at him. She picks up a lamp and launches it at him. It's still plugged in, so it doesn't go far.

"What the hell is going on down here?" Uncle Randy demands as he stumbles down the stairs in nothing but his boxers and rubbing at his eyes.

"I told you, Randy!" She points accusingly at us.

"They're fucking! It's incest."

Randy stills at the bottom of the stairs. "You caught them?"

"Look!" She waves her hand at us. "I interrupted something!"

"You're out of line," Hudson snaps. "We were going through our parents' things. That was all. Stop your horrible fucking accusations."

She rushes to Hudson and slaps his face. "Don't. Lie. To. Me." When she goes to slap him again, he grabs her wrist.

"Get the fuck away from me," he seethes, his shoulders tense with rage.

"Hudson," I whimper, willing him to calm down.

"Let her go," Uncle Randy barks, stalking over to us.

"Tell her to stop hitting me," Hudson snaps as he releases her.

She slaps him again. "I ought to kill you! Fucking your sister? You're a sick sonofabitch!"

"Aunt Becky!" I cry out. "Stop!"

She starts pummeling Hudson's chest with her fists. He grabs her forearms and holds her away from him.

"Get your goddamn hands off her, boy," Uncle Randy orders. He pulls her away from my brother and comes between them. "I think it's time for you to pack your shit and leave. You're causing too much trouble in my home."

"I'm causing trouble?" Hudson laughs scornfully. "Your meddling bitch of a wife is sticking her nose in places that are not her busin—"

His words get cut short when Uncle Randy shoves him. Hudson knocks into me and I hit the floor hard.

When Hudson realizes I've been pushed into the floor, he goes crazy and attacks our uncle. Hudson lands a punch, but Uncle Randy is scrappy. They scuffle and run into things. I scream at them to stop, but they don't listen.

"Please stop!" I beg through my tears as I scramble to my feet. "Aunt Becky, make them stop!" But she's gone. Left these two beasts to duke it out alone with me as their only spectator.

Hudson hits Uncle Randy in the ribs but then takes an elbow to the chin. As soon as I see blood dripping from Hudson's mouth, I grow dizzy. I stumble and crawl over to where Hudson and I were sitting only moments before. Drawing my knees to my chest, I bury my face to hide from their fighting. Tears stream endlessly down my cheeks. I rock back and forth, hoping for this to end soon.

Grunts.

Punches.

Furniture crashing.

It goes on forever.

Until people stomp down the stairs to join us. Police. The police are here. Nononononononono!

"Hudson," I whisper.

Two officers break up the fight and drag the men apart from each other. My eyes clash with Hudson's and heartbreak flashes across his features. This is the end. It all ends.

"He's been fucking his sister," Aunt Becky yells at them. "She's mentally ill. He took advantage of her."

"No," I croak out, sitting up on my knees. "No. You've got it all wrong."

"You're going to prison for fucking life," she hisses at him. "Say goodbye to her because this is the last you'll ever see of her."

"No!" I scream and run for him. I throw myself against him, but he's already handcuffed and can't hug me back.

"Don't arrest my brother! You can't take my brother!"

"Rylie," he chokes out.

One of the cops pulls me away from Hudson. Sobs wrack through me as they take him away from me.

"You'll never see her again," Aunt Becky hisses.

The room blurs as tears swim before me. I fall to the floor and cry hysterically. Aunt Becky tries to console me, but I kick away from her.

"Don't do this," I beg, my body shuddering. "Please."

She glowers at me. "It's been done. He's sick and now you're safe. I'll keep you safe. He'll never touch you again. I'll make sure he stays away for life."

Her words hit their intended mark and I shut down.

No.

I need him.

"We didn't do anything wrong," I whisper, my bottom lip wobbling wildly.

"He took advantage of you. I'm sorry, Rylie. Someone had to step in."

TWENTY-THREE

Hudson

I'm in a zone when I'm booked in the local jail. My thoughts circling around her. RylieRylieRylie. Is she okay? Is she crying? Fuck. I'm bruised and everything fucking hurts, but my heart aches so badly.

I can't do time.

I can't be away from her.

"One phone call," the deputy tells me.

Blinking away my daze, I follow him to the phone. With shaking hands, I dial a number I've had memorized since I was a teenager.

"Hello?"

"Amy. It's me, Hudson."

"Hudson? Why are you calling so late?"

"I need help. I need you to go get Rylie and keep her safe. Look out for her."

"Why? Where are you? What happened?"

I let out a sigh. "I'm at the jail for—"

"Don't say anything else," she interrupts. "Here, talk to Dad."

"Hello?" a sleepy voice greets.

"Mr. Kent." I pause. "I'm in jail."

"Shit, Hudson. What happened? Actually, don't say anything until I get there to represent you." I hear him shuffling. "'Tell them your attorney is on the way."

"I just wanted Amy to check on my sister. I didn't think—"

"Nothing else, son. Don't say anything."

Nodding, I choke back my emotion. "Thank you."

He hangs up and my heart feels heavy. Rylie won't take this well. I need Amy to check on her and make sure she's okay.

My mind is still a fog and it isn't until they've long shut the door behind me to a holding cell that I let it all sink in. It happened. No matter how hard we tried, the forces trying to pull us apart were stronger.

They won.

And we fucking lost.

Her cries of anguish gut me. They reverberate through the thin walls that separate our bedrooms and rattle their way into my soul.

They're dead. They're dead. They're fucking dead.

I've only been home for a few hours, but it's enough to realize Rylie is going to really need me. We lost our parents. She's already so fragile and broken. It'll be up to me to look after her because Mom and Dad can't.

I think about those times a few years ago when her depression got worse as puberty hit. Mom and Dad were always doing their best to console her. So many times she'd cry in her bed at night— times that used to annoy me. Looking back, I realize it was me who was wrong. In my shitty life where I have everyone convinced I have a plan and a future, nothing lives inside me. I'm empty.

Rylie's not empty.

She's filled with more emotions than a normal human can

manage. *Inside of her lives anger and sadness and despair. I should have been left with the happiness, but it would seem it's an elusive emotion the Hales aren't privy to.*

Mom and Dad were our happiness.

Those times when I felt like the pressure was too much, all it took was an encouraging, supportive phone call from Mom. A one or two-worded text from Dad that meant everything. They may not have been rich like Aunt Becky and Uncle Randy, but my parents did everything for us. Their entire world existed to provide us with not only a good, safe home and lifestyle, but also with unconditional love.

Rylie's wails grow louder.

Thump. Thump. Thump.

Something deep inside of me seems to wake from slumber.

Go to her. Make her happy. It's your duty.

I slide from my bed, alarmed at the way my chest throbs and my bones rattle. The overwhelming need to comfort her and show to her that we're not alone is pulsating through me. Slipping from my room, I quietly make it into hers as to not wake our aunt, who's sleeping in the living room. I push into my sister's room and close the door behind me.

"Rylie."

Her name is barely whispered from my lips, but it's powerful. It has the ability to turn her wails into whimpers. Her curses to God into prayers for me to hold her.

Purpose surges through my chest like never before.

Amy. Baseball. College.

Nothing has made me feel like I feel in this exact moment.

I lift the covers and she scoots over to give me room. Once I slide beneath the sheets, she claws desperately at me. Drawing her into my arms, I hug her to my bare chest. Her hair smells like lavender and it's a soothing scent—so different from Amy's expensive products I'm used to. I inhale my sister and run comforting circles with my fingertips along her back. Her tears soak my neck and chest, but they're subsiding.

It's up to me to heal her.

This is something I can do.

She settles and her breathing evens out. Pride thunders through me. I kiss her hair and hold her tight. In my arms, she doesn't feel like my sister. She feels like a tiny piece of the Hale heart that's left. My piece isn't much bigger now that our parents are gone. But together, we can be something. We can survive and fucking thrive. I just know it.

Her body feels so frail. I don't want her to break apart, so I hold her as close as I can, kissing her hair over and over again. We're pushed together, our bodies touching where they've never before touched, and it feels right. I've been such a selfish prick keeping my sister at a distance. All along, we could have been gaining strength from each other. I could have felt some peace when my world felt so fucking pointless—all I had to do was hold her.

As her breathing evens out finally and sleep steals her, I'm aware of how much my sister has grown into a woman. She'll be eighteen in a few months. It's strange to me to hold her so intimately. It makes me realize her body isn't much different than Amy's. Her breasts are soft pushed against me. Long, slender, smooth legs tangle with mine beneath the sheets. Our pelvises are pressed together, making my cock aware of our nearness. Very much a woman.

Images of her dating haunt me.

She doesn't need anyone in her fragile state.

Rylie just needs me to hold her. That's all she'll ever need.

My palm finds her ass over her shorts and I pull her closer. Images quick and dirty flit through my mind and it's a reprieve from the aching sadness I've been sucker punched with for the past few hours. As I drift to sleep, I allow myself to dwell in those thoughts. To blame my grief for wondering what our bodies would feel like naked and pressed together. Would we feel whole then?

My cock thinks so. I'm thankful she's asleep and doesn't notice my arousal. I'm dizzied and confused at my physiological response to her coupled with the dangerous path my mind has gone on. Is this what happens when someone loses two people they love? Do they lose their fucking mind?

"I'm sick." Her words are sleepy and uttered in a whisper. She grows tense as reality tries to steal her from her slumber.

I squeeze her ass and rub my length against her stomach, just once, murmuring soft assurances to her. The rigidness from her body melts away and she becomes soft again in my arms. Tomorrow, I'll blame my curious, needy touches on the despair, but tonight it seems to help make my world not so dark.

Seeking out her ear, hidden by her hair, I whisper, "I'm your cure."

She shivers and clutches on tightly.

I'm your cure.

"I'm your attorney. Anything you say to me is privileged information," Bradley Kent says from across the table. "Tell me all the details. Even the ones you're embarrassed of."

So he's heard.

"We got into a fight because they accused my sister and me of incest." I stare down at the table that's worn and dirty.

"Accused? Were the accusations true?"

My heart sinks. If he knows, Amy knows. Everyone knows. "Nope." Keeping my word to Rylie, I lift my gaze and pin him with a hard stare. "I fought with my uncle. That much I can't deny, but the things they're accusing me of are untrue."

His eyes that look exactly like Amy's widen in surprise. "Okay."

"We lost our parents and spend a lot of time consoling each other. But to accuse my sister and me of sleeping together is fucking ridiculous," I snap.

He holds up both hands in defense, even though I can see the relief in his stare. "I believe you. At this point, we're just waiting for them to press charges. You were in their home, so claiming self-defense is a moot point in someone else's home. But considering this would be your first offense, you won't be looking for more than a slap on the wrist."

I grit my teeth. "And their accusations?"

"If there were proof, which there won't be since it didn't happen, any judge with sense in his head would throw it out. Hearsay doesn't stand up in court." He frowns. "However, if there were to be any proof provided or testimonies..." he trails off. "You could be doing some hard time. Both of you could."

Nick.

Fuck.

He could open up a can of fucking worms just by mentioning his own accusations.

"No testimonies," I lie. "No proof."

"Good."

TWENTY-FOUR

Rylie

It's been done. He's sick and now you're safe. I'll keep you safe. He'll never touch you again. I'll make sure he stays away for life."

Aunt Becky's words play over and over again inside my head on repeat. Cruel and never-ending. For hours she's attempted to console me, but I want to be left alone. In his space. I pull on his favorite baseball hoodie, curl up on the floor clutching a picture of my family, and cry at the unfairness of it all.

Every. Single. Last. One. Of. Them.

All taken from me.

Aunt Becky comes down a lot to check on me and tries to get me to eat or drink. I can't answer her. I can't look at her. All I can do is wonder what I did to deserve a life like this.

I was happy.

All the pain and suffering caused by the turmoil of loving my brother when I wasn't supposed to had come to an end.

Because he loved me too.

I no longer had to hide in the darkness of my mind.

He was there to find me. To hold me. To kiss and make love to me.

Now he's gone.

"It's been done. He's sick and now you're safe. I'll keep you safe. He'll never touch you again. I'll make sure he stays away for life."

But what is my life without him in it?

Can I bear to be driven back into the darkness? A leper because of the way my heart bleeds for someone deemed untouchable? Two souls desperate for the other and life's the puppet master who says they can't be together.

Life's a bitch.

A bigger bitch than Aunt Becky.

If Mom were here, she'd be furious. I wasn't joking when I told Hudson she'd hit him with his baseball bat. But Mom always protected her kids. She loved us fiercely. I think she would have tried to understand. Dad might have been the one to make her see.

They wouldn't have sent the other half of my heart away.

My parents would have found a way for us to be a family. Just like they always found a way to pay for baseball and doctor bills. They were resourceful and protective.

Pain, unlike anything I've ever felt before, makes my stomach seize violently. I've long since thrown up the cake from last night. All I can do is hurt and shudder and shiver and beg.

"He'll never touch you again. I'll make sure he stays away for life."

Thoughts of Hudson locked away shred my heart. Someone so beautiful and loving doesn't deserve this. It's unfair.

Aunt Becky comes and goes once more, the worry evident in her eyes that match Mom's, as she attempts to get me to go to bed at least. Eat some toast at least. Drink some tea at least.

All I can do is stare vacantly at her.

My tears have no end.

They just fall and fall and fall.

And fall.

"Mommy," I sob, my finger caressing the side of her face through the glass in the frame. "Daddy."

When I look at my brother's happy grin, the crack that had been whittling itself through my heart finally succeeds. I'm torn in two, my soul seeping out and soaking into the carpet.

"I'll make sure he stays away for life."

The pain is too much. I'll never recover from this. I won't ever move on from him. He's my one true love and I don't give a fuck about society. Fucking hypocrites. People lie and cheat on their spouses. They abuse children. Fudge on their taxes. File bankruptcy and don't pay their bills. They hit the ones they love. Say cruel things to the ones they care about. They want equality for blacks and gays and women and transgenders and immigrants.

But this?

They can't fucking deal with this?

A brother and sister who are madly in love.

Sick and healed by one another.

Not hurting a goddamned person.

They find *this*—us—the stain on humanity they just can't get past? They create laws in Monfuckingtana that say people like us are doomed for prison for a hundred years? For what? Love.

Fuck them.

Fuck those hypocrites.

Liars and abusers.

Scammers.

Blind fucking masses who say what we have is disgusting and gross.

Fuck them!

I rise on shaky feet and throw a pile of boxes into the floor. I want to destroy everything. This house. This world. Everyone in it.

I hate them.

I hate them for preaching love and not following through.

If this world is full of them and they won't let me have the one thing that keeps me here, then they can fucking have it all.

"Why does our love story have to be a tragedy?"

"Mom and Dad's love story was a tragedy. I guess all the good ones are."

"Not ours, baby. Ours won't be a tragedy."

"Promise?"

"Promise."

Hudson. I'm sorry we didn't win. I'm sorry our love story was a tragedy too.

Falling to my knees, I sob as I open the small rectangular box. If Mom were here, she'd pull me in her arms and promise she'd fix it all. Her words always healed me in some way. They had power like Hudson's do.

Did.

He's gone.

"I'll make sure he stays away for life."

Nine hundred dollars' worth of metal shimmers in the overhead light. Beckons to me. Reveals an answer.

"Why does our love story have to be a tragedy?"

"I guess all the good ones are."

Sharp. Brilliant. A way out.

I pick them up and marvel at them. Slide my middle finger and thumb through the holes to learn the weight of them.

Snap. Snap. Snap.

I vividly remember visiting Mom at the shop as she snipped away at her clients' hair, making them go from sloppy to chic within minutes. She took something messy and made it beautiful.

Running my other thumb along the open blade of the scissors, I gasp. Crimson beads along the slice and I become transfixed on the way the blood drips on my bare thigh. Thighs that only hours ago were wrapped around Hudson.

I set the scissors down on the carpet and shove both my sleeves up. My arms are pale, but I can see the bluish veins beneath the surface. Is it that easy?

It will hurt.

My soul fucking hurts.

Anything would feel better than that.

I pick the scissors back up, this time holding them open, my palm digging into one of the blades. The bite of pain stings, but it isn't the worst in the world. I poke the tip of the other blade into my wrist. It doesn't puncture the skin, but when I drag it up my forearm, the skin opens up.

I remain still, staring at the bright red blood gushing from the line.

That didn't hurt.

No, the only thing that hurts is knowing I'll never see Hudson again.

That fucking hurts.

My hands begin to shake and my tears fall harder. With fumbling hands, I move the scissors into the other hand. The blade, this time, pokes harder and immediately breaks the skin. Burning pain tears along my flesh as the metal opens me up, but I don't hate it. I welcome the burn. I grow fixated on the blood.

It reminds me of when Hudson shaved my legs. When he accidentally cut my knee. His lips to my flesh gave me hope. Hope for a future and happiness. That small gift was a tiny seed that grew inside me. Nourished only by him. It grew and grew and grew and grew until it bloomed. Love. It bloomed into everlasting love.

And then they cut it.

Cut that hopeful, soul-rattling, blinding love from its source and stomped on it.

I was dead the moment they took him from me.

Sleepiness washes over me. I don't want to sleep, though. I want to stare at the beautiful blood that has colored my thighs and carpet. I want to use it to help me remember that time in the bathroom. I want to think of Hudson and him inside me.

Kissing and touching.

Not sick. Not wrong.

Love.

My head hits the carpet with a thunk and I have trouble keeping my eyes open.

I'll sleep now.

"What have you done?" he says, falling on his knees beside me. He's not here. He's not real. They've taken him away for life. That's what Aunt Becky said. "I'm here," he growls.

Blinking up at him, I smile. "I think I'm dying."

His perfect lips rain kisses down on me. Soft and worshipping. So Hudson. "You're not dying."

I hold up my bloody arm. The gash is gnarly. Open and

gushing. He tries to hold it closed. Hudson, my strong, beautiful brother, can't hold it closed. I'm too far gone.

"Every good love story ends in tragedy," I say.

"Ours wasn't supposed to."

He holds up the scissors, bright with my blood. "Show me how," he says.

I run my shaking, bloody finger along his forearm. "There."

Together, we stare in awe as he cuts open his flesh. Hudson doesn't want to be alone either. He wants to be with me.

Sick. Sick. Sick.

Together, we're healed.

He cuts the other side and then he bleeds. Pulls me to him and holds me close. Kisses my head and promises me our love won't end here.

A love like ours transcends the simple minds of those who occupy this world.

Our love is too powerful to exist in such a place.

"We're not a tragedy," Hudson says, his voice sleepy like mine.

Kiss. Kiss. Kiss.

Our mouths mate like our bodies no longer can.

"Look at us. We are." I laugh, but no one hears it. No one but Hudson. Like always.

"No." His voice is fierce, even though it's fading. "We're a happily ever after. Just a complicated one."

TWENTY-FIVE

Hudson

I've made bail.

Unreal.

Barely a night spent in jail. I was sure I'd spend the next decade or two locked away. Bradley told me I was looking at some time if they could somehow secure a testimonial. The claims of incest and assault would prove to be a violent concoction that could earn me many years. As I fell into a fitful sleep, worrying over Rylie, I'd come to accept my fate.

As long as the shit didn't touch Rylie, I'd do all the time required of me.

After I'm released, I walk into the lobby of the police station expecting to see Bradley. Instead, I find Uncle Randy. His face is swollen and bruised, but he isn't angry.

Sad.

His eyes are watery and filled with pain.

My anxiety spikes as my heart cracks.

"Rylie," I growl as I approach him.

He flinches at her name. Hot tears streak down my cheeks as I shove past him, desperate for air. As soon as I'm outside, I gasp in breaths as I hold on to a railing on the steps. My stomach clenches and my head spins.

"Listen," he says behind me.

"W-Where is s-she?" I can barely choke out the words.

"She's in the hospital."

Swiveling around, I grab him by his shirt. "Why? Why is she in the hospital?" I roar and shake him. "Why?"

He doesn't fight me, not like hours ago. Instead, a pained sound escapes him. "Jesus, Hudson. There was so much blood. I...I...she..." He swallows and his chin quivers. "She took your mom's scissors to her wrists. I swear we didn't know they were down there."

I did.

I knew.

My knees buckle and the world tilts on its axis. I hit the concrete painfully, my knees screaming as they're scraped and bruised through my sweatpants. I shudder and sob as I rip at my hair.

No.

Fucking no.

Why, Rylie?

I was always coming back to you. Eventually.

"Your aunt wants you to get up there," Uncle Randy says, his voice choked with emotion. "She thinks it'll do Rylie some good to see you."

I'm too weak and broken, but he grabs me from behind and lifts me to my feet. I lean on my uncle for strength as he walks us to the car. Both of us cry, uncaring if anyone judges us for it. Rylie needs me. I need her to fucking be okay.

"I, uh, we're not pressing charges," he says huskily.

Charges are the last thing I'm worried about. I simply nod as he pulls out onto the road. The drive to the hospital is short and the moment we arrive, I burst from the car, suddenly surging with newfound adrenaline. Uncle Randy hurries past me to show me where to go. When we arrive in a lobby, I find Amy sitting in a chair, her eyes red from crying.

"I'll text Becky. She's back there with her. They're only letting one person in at a time. I'll let her know you're here." He pulls out his phone and I pace the floor. "She says it will be a few minutes. I'll go grab us some coffee."

The moment he walks away, Amy lets out a ragged sob. "Oh, Hudson. Come here."

I crumple to my knees beside her and hug her waist. Amy and I may not be a couple anymore, but she's been a part of my family for years. Other than Rylie and my aunt and uncle, she's the closest person to me.

"I can't lose her," I rasp out. "I can't."

"Shhh," she says, stroking my hair. "You're not going to lose her. She's fine."

We're silent for a moment, her soft crying the only thing that can be heard.

"Hudson?"

I lift up and regard her, my eyes burning but no match for the pain inside my heart. "Yeah?"

"I wish you both the best."

I clench my jaw. "I just want my sister well."

Her bottom lip quivers. "You never looked at me the way you looked at her. I would never be able to compete with that."

I blink at her, my face becoming hard like stone. The tears don't get the memo and streak down my face.

"Don't say anything," she breathes. "Just know I may not understand the whys, but I do understand you. For the first time since I've known you, your eyes would sparkle. Your smile would be so wide it looked like it hurt." She sniffles. "Your eyes would track and follow her every move, as though the mere thought of her out of your sight was painful."

"She's my sister," I bite out, my words not holding venom. I'll never admit to what Rylie and I have. Not in a thousand years. It's our secret. Nobody has to know.

"I know…" she says. "I know you love her more than anything in this world. And what I'm trying and failing to say is, I want you to have that. I want you to be happy, Hudson."

"I just want to keep her safe."

She purses her lips together. "Then to keep her safe, you'll need to make a new life. Your life can't exist here where everyone knows you."

Gritting my teeth, I don't let on that her words are true.

"Room 305," Uncle Randy calls out from down the corridor.

I jerk to my feet and stalk away from my past toward my future.

Once I find the room, I knock. The door opens and Aunt Becky steps out. Her eyes are swollen from crying. As soon as she sees me, she yanks me to her and hugs me. I remain stiff in her arms.

"I need to see her," I choke out.

"I know you do, baby." She squeezes me tight and whispers, "I'm so sorry."

As soon as she pulls away, I slip past her into the room. Rylie is awake and staring at the ceiling. The door closes behind me. Quietly, I approach her bed. Her arms have been wrapped with white bandages, but blood is still in the crevices of her fingernails.

"I was always coming back for you, heathen," I whisper.

She flinches and turns her head. Her impassive features crumple as all the feelings at seeing me rush in. A loud sob hangs in her throat.

"Shhh," I coo as I sit on the bed next to her. My hand is gentle as I take hers in mine. "Don't ever fucking try to leave me alone again." She blurs as my tears leak out.

"I…I…thought they t-took you away f-forever," she sobs. "I couldn't live without you."

"I'm here, baby."

Needing to be closer to her, I twist my body and put my legs on the bed beside hers. I lay my head on her stomach and hug her to me.

"We're going to leave this place, Rylie. Just you and me. We don't belong here anymore. I'm not sure we ever did. But where we do belong is together." I kiss her stomach. "You can't hurt yourself, though. I won't fucking be able to deal with losing you. Promise me."

"I promise," she chokes out.

Her weak fingertips run through my hair and I close my eyes.

"We're not a goddamned tragedy."

"I know," she breathes. "We're a happily ever after. Just a complicated one."

Two months later…

"Are you sure this is a good idea?" Aunt Becky asks, a frown marring her features.

"She needs the vacation. And then…"

She sighs. "I know. I just…I hate to see you both go."

I hug my aunt and let out a heavy breath. "She needs a change of scenery. I'll always take care of her." I pull away and start for the truck that's packed with our luggage where

Rylie's already waiting inside. Finally, after weeks and weeks of physical therapy from the damage she inflicted on herself, the doctor says she's on the mend and safe to do normal things. While she missed vital veins when she cut herself, she did a number on her muscles, nerves, and ligaments. But she's worked hard to get where she is now. A long overdue vacation is in order.

"Hudson," Aunt Becky calls out.

"Yeah?"

"Just so you know, this isn't me condoning…you know."

Incest?

I grin at my aunt. "I have no idea what you're talking about." To this day, Rylie and I deny it. Even when Aunt Becky finds us glued together, clinging desperately to each other in our sleep in her downstairs basement.

She cracks a rare smile. "You're a little asshole like your mom."

"I'll take that as a compliment, Aunt Becky."

I climb into the truck and wave at her as she goes back inside. Rylie reaches over and holds her palm out to me, her long rosy-pink scar visible on her forearm that no longer dons bandages. I take my ring from her palm and slide it on my finger before kissing the side of her head.

"Can we make a couple of pit stops along the way?" she asks, her hand settling on my thigh as we pull out onto the road.

"Yeah. Where are we headed?"

"I need to see Travis."

I arch a brow and shoot her a questioning look.

She grins at me—bright and beautiful. "You're not jealous, are you?"

"Jealous of that fucker? Hell no." I grunt because even

though I'm twice his size and my cock is no doubt bigger, it still bugs me she needs to see him.

"I promise it will be fine. And then I want to go to Eureka Springs."

"You do realize that's in Arkansas," I say with a huff.

"Yep."

"Four and a half hours south."

"I know where it's at," she sasses.

Goddamn it's wonderful hearing the real Rylie again. I thought I lost her. These past two months helping her find herself have been trying. She's been frustrated at not being able to do simple tasks like dress and fix her hair. Luckily, she has me. And I know how to shave her legs for her, too.

"Lake of the Ozarks is only an hour and a half away," I complain.

She laughs. "Just go with it, Hudson."

With a smile that exactly matches hers, because we're siblings and all, I do as she wishes. She's practically jumping out of her skin when we pull into Travis's driveway. When she starts fishing through her wallet and pulls out a wad of cash, unease skitters through me.

"Where'd you get all that money?" I demand.

She scrunches her nose up as she frowns. "Aunt Becky gave me money for my graduation."

"And why are you about to give it to Travis of all fucking people?"

She turns her head and parts her lips. "You'll see. Wait here."

I press a kiss to her pouty mouth and watch her climb out of the truck. Today she's wearing a simple white dress with sandals. Her dark hair is down and hangs in smooth chocolate waves. She's gone for about five minutes and then she comes bounding down the stairs with a huge grin on her face, a yellow envelope in her hand.

"To Eureka Springs," she says as she buckles in beside me.

As we drive, I wrap my arm around her and hug her to my side. "What's in Eureka Springs anyway?"

She rests her head on me. "It's where Mom and Dad got married. I always wanted to get married there too."

Guilt sluices through me. Some things I'll never be able to give her. "Ry—"

"I worked it all out, Hudson. Don't worry."

She seems so happy and sure of herself. I'll be damned if I rain on her parade. "What's in the envelope, heathen?"

"Everything we need to change our future."

Turns out, everything we needed was a new fake ID, birth certificate, and social security card. Heather Miller. The woman I legally married—or illegally depending on how you look at it—in a whimsical forest in Eureka Springs, Arkansas.

"Tell me you're happy," she says as we walk up to the treehouse cabin hidden in a thicket of trees. "Please tell me you're okay with this."

I hook her waist with my arm and pull her against me. Not even an hour ago, I pledged my loyalty and love to her until death do us part. The ordained minister was an old man with bifocals an inch thick and who could hardly hear a thing. He didn't correct us when I vowed to Rylie *not Heather* that I'd love her through sickness, especially through sickness. Being allowed to say my vows to her meant the world to me. And seeing the happiness shining in her wide brown eyes meant she loved it too.

"I'm so happy," I tell her, kissing the top of her head. "Now let's go check out this place you secretly booked using *my* credit card."

She laughs as we climb the steps. It's high up in the trees. Such a cool fucking place nestled in the middle of nowhere. When we get to the top, she unlocks the door, but I don't let her enter the cabin.

"Not yet, wife," I growl.

She squeals when I scoop her into my arms and carry her over the threshold. "You're so romantic, husband."

We both chuckle because it'll take some getting used to calling each other those names.

I kick the door closed behind me and set her to her feet. The space is quaint with lots of windows but furnished with a modern flare.

"A heart-shaped bathtub?" I ask with a laugh.

"Shush, it's cute."

She runs over to the bathtub that's situated in an alcove on the other side of the king-sized bed and sits on the edge. It's surrounded by windows that overlook the dense forest below. "It's beautiful."

I stand behind her and run my fingers through her soft hair. "It is."

She turns to face me and stares up at me with so much fucking devotion in her eyes it hurts. "I like it here. Maybe we could…"

I know what she wants. I feel it running through me as well. "Stay here and make new vacation memories?"

She bites on her bottom lip and nods as though she's worried I'll tell her no. I'll never tell her no. Not ever. Rylie will have whatever she wants in this life. I will see to it that she does. That's all *I* want.

I cup her cheeks and bend over to kiss her lips. "Yes. Let's do it."

She launches herself into my arms. I grab her ass and hoist her skinny body up. Our mouths crash together as I guide her over to the bed. Gently, I drop her to the mattress but then make haste at pulling off her white dress. I'm careful of her arms that are still healing. Even though the stiches are out and the wounds have healed, she still has a lot of pain not only to the touch but when she uses her arms too much.

"Look at you," I say as I take a minute to admire her in her sexy undergarments. Hale, in my signature, is scrawled across her ribs in harsh black ink, claiming her as mine. The wedding band glimmers in the sunlight pouring in through the windows behind me.

"Look at you," she replies, a smile on her lips. Then, she unhooks her bra from behind and frees her perky tits. The nipples are hard and at attention, just begging for my teeth.

I reach forward and pull her sandals off one by one, letting them clatter to the wood floors. She lies back and stares at me with desire swimming in her eyes. My cock aches in my shorts. We haven't fucked much in the past two months. Having gone through all the shit we did with Aunt Becky finding out, we've made sure to only have sex when we knew they were at work and not in the house. I'm eager to have her today and by the sultry look on her face, I'd say she's more than ready to have me too.

"Take off your panties," I instruct.

She slides her feet to the bed and lifts her ass so she can push her panties down. I lean forward and grab the lacy material to help them down her thighs. Once she's naked and bared to me, I push her knees apart. In the bright sunshine, her cunt is pale pink and glistening.

I reach behind my neck and tug off my shirt. The rest of my clothes get shed quickly. Her features become dark and hungry as she stares at my cock that bounces out in front of me. I kneel on the side of the bed and grab her hips. She laughs when I jerk her to the edge so her ass hangs off. Her laughter dies in her throat, though, when I run my tongue along her juicy slit. Her back arches up off the bed, making her tits jiggle.

"Hudson," she begs.

I make work at sucking on her clit. I love the way it makes her squeal and squirm and scream. It doesn't take long before she's coming unglued as her orgasm takes over. She's still shaking when I pounce on her. Sliding my arm beneath her, I pull her farther up the bed. She whimpers when my cock rubs against her sensitive clit.

"You want my cock inside you, heathen? Did you miss it stretching your tight little hole?"

"Oh God," she moans. "Yes. I need you."

With a grin, I grab my dick and guide it into her waiting body. We both let out a hiss of air as I push my cock inside her to the hilt. Several times, I slide in and out slowly so I can watch the way my body fits inside hers. The way her pussy seems stretched to the limits. How her arousal coats my dick and lubricates it.

"Look at how perfect we fit," I mutter, my eyes fixated on where we're joined. "Do you see?"

She bites on her bottom lip and nods as she watches me fuck her. "It feels good too."

"Feels really fucking good," I agree.

I settle on top of her tiny body so I can look in her eyes. Hers shine with love and adoration. The feeling is mutual. I thread my fingers in her hair and kiss her mouth as my hips thrust against her. I'll never be able to fathom how I lived without having Rylie like this. We're two halves of a heart that only beats together.

"Hudson," she cries out against my mouth.

I slide my palm to her ribs that feel breakable under my hand but somehow also strong with Hale scrawled across them. "Rylie."

Fragments of words mixed with moans echo in the tree-house cabin. Our sweaty bodies are slick as we fuck. Each of us desperately clinging to the other.

She murmurs words of love and praise. I show her with my body that I feel the same.

Together, we make sweet, frantic love.

She's my wife—my sister—my everything.

Life may feel too short and too fragile…

I'll be damned if I waste one second of it.

TWENTY-SIX

Rylie

Several months later...

"I can get it," I grumble, even though I worry about my arms giving out. My new doctor says I have nerve damage that may never heal back up. Dreams of cutting hair like Mom did were pushed aside as I had to discover my own strengths and abilities.

Hudson ignores me as he uses the oven mitts to pull out the giant turkey from the oven. He sets it on the stovetop and then closes the door. "Doesn't look like Mom's," he muses aloud.

I swat at him. "It's a new recipe." I nudge him with my hip and he steps out of the way, but not before sticking his finger in the mashed potatoes. "Don't you have work to do?"

He grins at me, wide and boyish. After all this time together, as a couple, it's still hard to believe he's mine. "Boyd says everyone deserves Thanksgiving off."

I shake my head. "He did not say that."

Hudson runs the books for Boyd Williams' riverside resort. His cabins are top-of-the-line and have the best views in Jasper. He also lets us rent one of the cabins in a secluded section of his property for hardly anything. I may not know much about finance and accounting like my genius brother, but Boyd lets me help with marketing and website stuff. He's been patient and so nice to take us under his wing.

"He said, and I quote, 'Enjoy the day off, watch some football, eat some peeh-can pie, make a turd, and give yer wife some lovin'. But not in that order, son. Definitely not in that order.'"

I giggle because I can imagine Boyd saying just that. His belly is big, but his handlebar mustache is bigger. Funniest country bumpkin you'll ever meet. Probably the richest one in Jasper, Arkansas too. His wife, Patty, should have earned a medal for putting up with him for thirty years. "That sounds like the Boyd I know."

Hudson laughs as he roots around in the fridge, no doubt after the devilled eggs I made earlier. Memories of Mom cracking him with the towel for eating her dinner before it was ready have me smiling. I don't fuss at him but instead make sure everything is ready to eat.

"You want to say the blessing?" I ask as I pull off my apron. The first Thanksgiving without our parents is hard, but Hudson promised me we'll make new memories. Always making new memories. This is how we move forward.

He walks up behind me, resting his chin on my head, and palms my stomach. "Lord, thank you for giving us each other and this perfect life in Jasper. Tell Mom and Dad hi."

I laugh and swat at his hand. "And?"

"Thank you for letting Rylie make me food all the time now, Lord. I'm *extra* nice to her."

"All you had to do was say please. I told you this when we were kids. You were just too stubborn back then," I say with a playful huff.

We both chuckle.

"And what else?" I ask.

"Thank you, Lord, for blessing this food."

"Amen," I say primly.

He kisses the side of my neck. "Is my son hungry?"

As if woken up by his daddy, our son kicks at him.

"Always." Turning, I slide my palms up Hudson's firm chest and rest them on his shoulders. My stomach is round and large between us. Life is pretty perfect.

"Did you take your medicine?" he murmurs, his dark brows furrowed in concern.

Well, almost perfect.

My new doctor in Jasper has prescribed antidepressants that are safe during pregnancy since my old ones were not. I don't like taking them, but I also don't like how low and dark my mind can get. The medicine helps keep me on the straight and narrow. But Hudson is the one who heals me altogether.

His love is a cure.

"I did. Do you think…" I trail off and bite on my bottom lip, hoping to keep the tears at bay. "Do you think he'll be like me?"

Hudson tangles his fingers in my hair and kisses me fiercely. When I'm gasping for air, he pulls away and rests his forehead to mine. "I hope he's just like you. Smart. Perfect. A great cook. Funny. Fucking adorable."

I grin at him. "Maybe I want him to be like you. Strong and a math whiz."

"That's it? I give you five things and you give me two?" His teeth nip playfully at my jaw and the side of my neck.

"You're a lot more than two," I agree. My smile falls. "I meant, you know, mentally ill."

No matter how many times Hudson assures me our son will be fine, I worry. There's a chance that, genetically, I could pass down my depression to my son. But what I worry most about is new illnesses given to him because of who his father is—*my brother*. I've scoured the Internet looking for articles about incest. Despite the hate and disgust geared toward the subject, I've yet to find any proof that birth defects and mental disorders are linked to incest. In my effort to find answers, though, I did find a forum where people like us from all over the world have a place to discuss our challenges and triumphs while remaining anonymous. The admins of the group monitor the people in it closely and keep any hate away from us. I've found a friend, Maggie, who's also with her brother. They have three kids and all of them are healthy. I ask her millions of questions and she answers them all patiently.

"Do you remember our vows?" he asks, his lips trailing kisses along my cheek until he reaches my mouth.

"I love you, even in sickness, Rylie. I'll do the same for our son. We're a family."

Blinking away my tears, I smile at him. "A family."

"Now let's see if this dinner turned out okay. It's not too late to crash Boyd and Patty's dinner if it's a total fail," he teases, lightening the mood.

"You're an asshole," I grumble, unable to hide my smile.

"An asshole who was inside your asshole last night, heathen." He grins wickedly at me.

"Hudson Hale!"

"Yes, Rylie Hale?"

"You're so bad."

He laughs, the sound deep and rumbly. "Then you must be bad too because you came loud enough that I was sure half the guests down the river heard me stretching out your needy little asshole."

I shake my head at him. "This is not a good start to our

official first Thanksgiving."

"Whatever you say, beautiful. I think it's kind of perfect." He steals a kiss as he sets to cutting up the turkey.

I pick up the bowl of mashed potatoes and only wince slightly at the pain that shoots up my arms. I've been working hard with the weights lately because I want to be able to carry my son with no problems. One day soon, I hope to have full, pain-free functionality of my arms.

As we settle at our two-person table that already has a high chair set up and waiting nearby, I take a moment to enjoy our little slice of heaven. Beyond the big window that faces the west is an endless sea of trees, all of which are brilliant oranges, yellows, reds, and browns. The beautiful and winding Buffalo River can be seen cutting through the trees down below.

Hudson reaches across the table and runs his fingertip along my scar on my right arm. I turn to regard him, marveling at how handsome he is. He's let his scruff grow in and it makes him seem older and more rugged.

Mine.

"I couldn't ask for anything more than this, Rylie. This is everything." His hand clutches mine. "*You* are everything."

EPILOGUE

Hudson

Six and a half years later...

"Run, JJ, run!" Rylie hollers from the picnic table where she sits with Aunt Becky.

Our son runs as fast as his little legs will take him around the makeshift bases. His slightly older cousin, Hunter, finds the baseball and lobs it at Uncle Randy, who misses. Hunter and Uncle Randy can't play baseball for shit, but they're still all smiles. When JJ stomps on home base, he runs over to me and throws his skinny arms around my waist.

"Home run, Daddy," he says, panting.

His dark hair is sweaty and slightly curly. Cutest damn boy on the planet. Looks just like his grandpa Jerald James Hale who he's named after.

"Good job, squirt," I tell him and then ruffle his hair.

"Can we go swimming now?" he asks, no longer interested in our baseball game. We rode on the boat all afternoon then stopped for lunch and a quick game of baseball.

"Swimming!" Lo, short for Lauren after her grandma, hollers, waving her chunky arms in the air.

Rylie scoops up our three-year-old daughter, who's been playing in the sand near the picnic table, and hefts her on her hip. She may be pregnant with our third child, but she still looks as beautiful as ever. When our eyes catch, hers beam with happiness. I know mine reflect the same.

Aunt Becky, finally pregnant with their second, waddles behind Rylie. Her cheeks are full and her face is red, but my grumpy Aunt Becky is much calmer these days. After Rylie nearly taking her life, something shifted in our aunt. It was never spoken about. To this day, we keep up the lie that Travis keeps knocking up *Rylie Hale.* Such a deadbeat dad. Poor Travis.

But Heather Miller?

Heather Miller, according to the state of Arkansas, married Hudson Hale on a hot, late summer day. They honeymooned for a full week in a treehouse cabin in Eureka Springs. Then, they took to the road and settled in the first town that felt like home. Jasper, Arkansas. Hudson Hale bumped into a feisty old man with a handlebar mustache arguing over his change in a corner store. He sorted the old man out and the man offered him a job, a home, and a slice of paradise. Hudson Hale is listed as the father on both JJ and Lo's birth certificates. And when baby Colin arrives, his will look the same.

And to further extend the lie, we told Aunt Becky and Uncle Randy the kids would call me Daddy so they wouldn't know their real dad was a piece of shit. A *fake* piece of shit, but a piece of shit nonetheless.

Our aunt and uncle don't argue with us. They don't call us out on our lies. They don't ask questions. And they certainly don't look at us with disgust like I thought they might. Instead, they simply beg us to keep in touch and spend at least one week during the summer at Lake of the Ozarks with them.

Near the water's edge, I help JJ put his lifejacket back on. Once he's strapped up, he follows Hunter and Uncle

Randy onto the boat, always eager to spend time with his cousin and uncle. Aunt Becky smiles at me as Uncle Randy helps her on the boat as well. Rylie and I linger for a moment. Her big brown eyes burn into mine, begging for a kiss.

But not here.

Not now.

Not outside of our safe bubble in the Ozark Mountains back in Jasper.

Tonight, though, when the kids are asleep and we're all alone, I'll kiss her all night. Everywhere. For as long as she asks me to.

"Off," Lo whines. She tries to tug at her lifejacket that we don't take off, even for lunch, but I tickle her and distract her. She reaches for me and grins, her toothy mouth adorable as hell. "Daddy."

Pulling her to me, I kiss her soft brown hair and wink at Rylie, who stares at me with hungry eyes. "Later, heathen. I know what you want and you can have it later when no prying eyes are around. I promise."

An airplane passes overhead, gaining everyone's attention. The boys and our daughter are pointing in the sky. Uncle Randy and Aunt Becky are shielding their eyes as they look too.

"Nobody has to know," Rylie murmurs, biting on her succulent bottom lip that I know will taste just like the watermelon she's been nibbling on all day.

Leaning in, I steal a kiss because she's impossible to deny.

Quick. Sweet. Ours.

"You taste like watermelon and happiness," I say as we walk toward the boat. I give her butt a discreet squeeze over her swimsuit that hugs her perfect ass. It's plumped out again now that she's pregnant and I love it. *Nobody has to know.*

She grins back at me. "You taste like mine."

The End

(A happily ever after. Just a complicated one.)

PLAYLIST

Listen on Spotify

"High and Dry" by Radiohead

"True Love is Violent" by Allie X

"Breathe" by Fleurie

"Meet Me on the Battlefield" by Svrcina

"Walk Through the Fire" by Zayde Wolf and Ruelle

"Wildest Ones" by Zayde Wolf

"Simon Says" by Allie X

"Riptide" by Vancy Joy

"Good Vibrations" by The Beach Boys

"Feel It Still" by Portugal The Man

"Radioactive" by Imagine Dragons

"Not Your Fault" by AWOLNATION

"Renegades" by X Ambassadors

"Put the Gun Down" by ZZ Ward

"Stuck In The Middle With You" by Stealers Wheel

"Sweater Weather" by The Neighbourhood

"Cough Syrup" by Young the Giant

"Love is Mystical" by Cold War Kids

"Never Be the Same" by Camila Cabello

"Happy Pills" by Weathers

"Lonely Boy" by The Black Keys

"Clocks" by Coldplay

"Everybody Hurts" by R.E.M.

"I Found" by Amber Run

"Control" by Halsey

"Paper Love" by Allie X

"Can You Hold Me" by NF and Britt Nicole

"Way Down We Go" by Kaleo

"Glory and Gore" by Lorde

"A Little Wicked" by Valerie Broussard

"Daddy Issues" by The Neighborhood

"Idfc" by Blackbear

"i hate u, i love u" by gnash and Olivia O'Brien

"Like Lovers Do" by Hey Violet

"Desire" by Meg Myers

BOOKS BY
K WEBSTER

The Breaking the Rules Series:
Broken (Book 1)
Wrong (Book 2)
Scarred (Book 3)
Mistake (Book 4)
Crushed (Book 5 – a novella)

The Vegas Aces Series:
Rock Country (Book 1)
Rock Heart (Book 2)
Rock Bottom (Book 3)

The Becoming Her Series:
Becoming Lady Thomas (Book 1)
Becoming Countess Dumont (Book 2)
Becoming Mrs. Benedict (Book 3)

War & Peace Series:
This is War, Baby (Book 1)—BANNED
(only sold on K Webster's website)
This is Love, Baby (Book 2)
This Isn't Over, Baby (Book 3)
This Isn't You, Baby (Book 4)
This is Me, Baby (Book 5)
This Isn't Fair, Baby (Book 6)
This is the End, Baby (Book 7 – a novella)

2 Lovers Series:
Text 2 Lovers (Book 1)
Hate 2 Lovers (Book 2)
Thieves 2 Lovers (Book 3)

Alpha & Omega Duet:
Alpha & Omega (Book 1)
Omega & Love (Book 2)

Pretty Little Dolls Series:
Pretty Stolen Dolls (Book 1)
Pretty Lost Dolls (Book 2)
Pretty New Doll (Book 3)
Pretty Broken Dolls (Book 4)

The V Games Series:
Vlad (Book 1)

Taboo Treats:
Bad Bad Bad
Easton
Crybaby
Lawn Boys
Malfeasance
Renner's Rules

Carina Press Books:
Ex-Rated Attraction
Mr. Blakely

Four Fathers Books:
Pearson

Standalone Novels:

Apartment 2B

Love and Law

Moth to a Flame

Erased

The Road Back to Us

Surviving Harley

Give Me Yesterday

Running Free

Dirty Ugly Toy

Zeke's Eden

Sweet Jayne

Untimely You

Mad Sea

Whispers and the Roars

Schooled by a Senior

B-Sides and Rarities

Blue Hill Blood by Elizabeth Gray

Notice

The Wild – BANNED (only sold on K Webster's website)

The Day She Cried

My Torin

El Malo

Sunshine and the Stalker

Sundays are for Hangovers

Hale

ACKNOWLEDGEMENTS

Thank you to my husband. You're my biggest supporter and my inspiration. I love you madly, my dear.

A huge thank you to my Krazy for K Webster's Books reader group. You all are insanely supportive and I can't thank you enough.

A gigantic thank you to those who helped me with this book. Elizabeth Clinton, Ella Stewart, Misty Walker, Holly Sparks, Jillian Ruize, and Gina Behrends—you ladies are my rock!

A big thank you to my author friends who have given me your friendship and your support. You have no idea how much that means to me.

Thank you to all of my blogger friends both big and small that go above and beyond to always share my stuff. You all rock! #AllBlogsMatter

Emily A. Lawrence, thank you SO much for editing this book. You're a rock star and I can't thank you enough! Love you!

Thank you Stacey Blake for being amazing as always when formatting my books and in general. I love you! I love you! I love you!

A big thanks to my PR gal, Nicole Blanchard. You are fabulous at what you do and keep me on track!

Lastly but certainly not least of all, thank you to all of the wonderful readers out there who are willing to hear my story and enjoy my characters like I do. It means the world to me!

ABOUT
K WEBSTER

K Webster is the *USA Today* bestselling author of over sixty romance books in many different genres including contemporary romance, historical romance, paranormal romance, dark romance, romantic suspense, taboo romance, and erotic romance. When not spending time with her hilarious and handsome husband and two adorable children, she's active on social media connecting with her readers.

Her other passions besides writing include reading and graphic design. K can always be found in front of her computer chasing her next idea and taking action. She looks forward to the day when she will see one of her titles on the big screen.

Join K Webster's newsletter to receive a couple of updates a month on new releases and exclusive content. To join, all you need to do is go here (www. authorkwebster.com).

Facebook: www.facebook.com/authorkwebster

Blog: authorkwebster.wordpress.com

Twitter: twitter.com/KristiWebster

Email: kristi@authorkwebster.com

Goodreads: www.goodreads.com/user/show/10439773-k-webster

Instagram: instagram.com/kristiwebster

www.ingramcontent.com/pod-product-compliance
Lightning Source LLC
La Vergne TN
LVHW021953020125
800330LV00002B/329